The Greatest
Brazilian Holiday
Stories of
All Time

NEW VESSEL PRESS
NEW YORK

www.newvesselpress.com

Cover design by Sandra Jávera
Book design by Beth Steidle

Library of Congress Cataloging-in-Publication Data
Various
A Very Brazilian Christmas: The Greatest Brazilian Holiday Stories of All Time / various authors.
p. cm.
ISBN 978-1-954404-38-0
Library of Congress Control Number: 2025938655
I. Brazil—Fiction

Table of Contents

A VERY BRAZILIAN CHRISTMAS

Midnight Mass

Joaquim Maria Machado de Assis

I've never quite understood a conversation I had with a lady many years ago, when I was seventeen and she was thirty. It was Christmas Eve. Having arranged to attend midnight mass with a neighbor, I had agreed that I would stay awake and call for him just before midnight.

The house where I was staying belonged to the notary Meneses, whose first wife had been one of my cousins. His second wife, Conceição, and her mother had both welcomed me warmly when, months before, I arrived in Rio de Janeiro from Mangaratiba to study for my university entrance exams. I led a very quiet life in that two-story house on Rua do Senado, with my books, a few friends, and the occasional outing. It was a small household, consisting of the notary, his wife, his mother-in-law, and two slave-women. They kept to the old routines, retiring to bed at ten and with everyone sound asleep by half-past. Now, I had never been to the theater, and more than once, on hearing Meneses announce that he was going, I would ask him to take me with him. On such occasions, his mother-in-law would pull a disapproving face, and the slave-women would titter; he, however, would not even reply, but would get dressed, leave the house, and not return until the following morning. Only later on did I realize that the theater was a euphemism in action. Meneses was having an affair with a lady who was separated from her husband and, once a week, he slept elsewhere. At first Conceição had found the existence of this mistress deeply wounding, but, in the end, she had resigned herself and grown accustomed to the situation, deciding that there was nothing untoward about it at all.

Good, kind Conceição! People called her "a saint," and she did full justice to that title, given how easily she put up with her husband's neglect. Hers was a very moderate nature, with no extremes, no tearful tantrums, and no great outbursts of hilarity. In this respect, she would have been fine as a Muslim woman and would have been quite happy in a harem, as long as appearances were maintained. May God forgive me if I'm misjudging her, but everything about her was contained and passive. Even her face was average, neither pretty nor ugly. She was what people call "a nice person." She never spoke ill of anyone and was very forgiving. She wouldn't have known how to hate anyone, nor, perhaps, how to love them.

On that particular Christmas Eve, the notary went off to the theater. It was around 1861 or 1862. I should have been in Mangaratiba on holiday, but I had stayed until Christmas because I wanted to see what midnight mass was like in the big city. The family retired to bed at the usual time, and I waited in the front room, dressed and ready. From there I could go out into the hallway and leave the house without disturbing anyone. There were three keys to the front door: the notary had one, I would take the second, and the third would remain in the house.

"But Senhor Nogueira, what will you do to fill the time?" Conceição's mother asked.

"I'll read, Dona Inácia."

I had with me a novel, *The Three Musketeers*, in an old translation published, I think, by the *Jornal do Commercio*. I sat down at the table in the middle of the room, and by the light of an oil lamp, while the rest of the house was sleeping, I once again climbed onto D'Artagnan's scrawny horse and set off on an adventure. I was soon completely intoxicated by Dumas. The minutes flew past, as they so rarely do when one is waiting; I heard the clock strike eleven, but barely took any notice, as if it were of no importance. However, the sound of someone stirring in the house roused me from my reading: footsteps in the passageway between the parlor and the dining room. I looked up and, soon afterward, saw Conceição appear in the doorway.

"Still here?" she asked.

"Yes, it's not yet midnight."

"Such patience!"

Conceição came into the room, her bedroom slippers flip-flapping. She was wearing a white dressing gown, loosely tied at the waist. She was quite thin, and this somehow lent her a romantic air, rather in keeping with my adventure story. I closed the book, and she went and sat on the chair next to mine, near the couch. When I asked if I had unwittingly woken her by making a noise, she immediately said:

"No, not at all. I simply woke up."

I looked at her and rather doubted the truth of this. Her eyes were not those of someone who had been asleep, but of someone who had not yet slept at all. However, I quickly dismissed this observation—which might have borne fruit in someone else's mind—never dreaming that I might be the reason she hadn't gone to sleep and that she was lying so as not to worry or annoy me. She was, as I said, a kind person, very kind.

"It must be nearly time, though," I said.

"How do you have the patience to stay awake while your neighbor sleeps? And to wait here all alone too. Aren't you afraid of ghosts? I bet I startled you just now."

"I was a little surprised when I heard footsteps, but then you appeared immediately afterward."

"What were you reading? Don't tell me, I know: it's *The Three Musketeers*."

"Exactly. It's such a good book."

"Do you like novels?"

"I do."

"Have you read *The Dark-Haired Girl*?"

"By Macedo? Yes, I have it at home in Mangaratiba."

"I love novels, but I don't have much time to read anymore. What novels have you read?"

I began listing a few titles. Conceiçao listened, leaning her head against the chair back, looking at me fixedly through half-closed eyelids. Now and then, she would run her tongue over her lips to moisten them. When I finished speaking, she said nothing, and we sat in silence for a few seconds. Then, still gazing at me with her large, intelligent eyes, she sat up straight, interlaced her fingers, and rested her chin on them, her elbows on the arms of the chair.

"Perhaps she's bored," I thought. Then, out loud, I said:

"Dona Conceição, I think it must be nearly time, and I—"

"No, no, it's still early. I just looked at the clock and it's only half-past eleven. You still have time. If you ever do miss a night's sleep, can you get through the next day without sleeping at all?"

"I have in the past."

"I can't. If I miss a night's sleep, I'm no use for anything the next day and have to have a nap, even if it's only for half an hour. But then I'm getting old."

"What do you mean, 'old,' Dona Conceição?"

I spoke these words with such passion that it made her smile. She usually moved very slowly and serenely, but now she sprang to her feet, walked over to the other side of the room, and paced up and down between the window looking out onto the street and the door of her husband's study. Her modestly rumpled appearance made a singular impression on me. Although she was quite slender, there was something about that swaying gait, as if she were weighed down by her own body; I had never really noticed this until then. She paused occasionally to examine the hem of a curtain or to adjust the position of some object on the sideboard; finally, she stopped in front of me, with the table between us. Her ideas appeared to be caught in a very narrow circle; she again remarked on her astonishment at my ability to stay awake; I repeated what she already knew, that I had never attended midnight mass in Rio and did not want to miss it.

"It's just the same as mass in the countryside, well, all masses are alike, really."

"I'm sure you're right, but here it's bound to be more lavish and there'll be more people too. After all, Holy Week is much prettier in Rio than it is in the countryside. Not to mention the feasts of Saint John or Saint Anthony . . ."

She gradually leaned forward, resting her elbows on the marble tabletop, her face cupped in her outspread hands. Her unbuttoned sleeves fell back to reveal her forearms, which were very pale and plumper than one might have expected. This was not exactly a novelty, although it wasn't a common sight, either; at that moment, however, it made a great impression on me. Her veins were so blue that, despite the dim light, I could count every one. Her presence was even better at keeping me awake than my book. I continued to compare religious festivals in the countryside and in the city, and to give my views on whatever happened to pop into my head. I kept changing the subject for no reason, talking about one thing, then going back to something I'd mentioned earlier, and laughing in the hope that this would make her smile, too, thus affording me a glimpse of her perfect, gleaming white teeth. Her eyes were very dark, almost black; her long, slender, slightly curved nose gave her face an interrogative air. When I raised my voice a little, she told me off:

"*Ssh!* You might wake Mama!"

Much to my delight, though, she didn't move from where she was, our faces very close. It really wasn't necessary to speak loudly in order to be heard; we were both whispering, I even more softly than her, because I was doing most of the talking. At times, she would look serious—very serious—even frowning slightly. She eventually grew tired and changed position and place. She walked around to my side of the table and sat down on the couch. I turned and could just see the toes of her slippers, but only for the time it took her to sit down, because her dressing gown was long enough to cover them. I remember that the slippers were black. She said very softly:

"Mama's room is quite some way away, but she sleeps so very lightly, and if she were to wake up now, it would take her ages to get back to sleep."

"I'm the same."

"What?" she asked, leaning forward to hear better.

I went and sat on the chair beside the couch and repeated what I'd said. She laughed at the coincidence of there being three light sleepers in the same house.

"Because I'm just like Mama sometimes: if I do wake in the night, I find it hard to go back to sleep, I toss and turn, get up, light a candle, pace up and down, get into bed again, but it's no use."

"Is that what happened tonight?"

"No, not at all," she said.

I couldn't understand why she denied this, and perhaps she couldn't, either. She picked up the two ends of her dressing-gown belt and kept flicking them against her knees, or, rather, against her right knee, because she had crossed her legs. Then she told some story about dreams and assured me that she had only ever had one nightmare, when she was a child. She asked if I ever had nightmares. The conversation continued in this same slow, leisurely way, and I gave not a thought to the time or to mass. Whenever I finished some anecdote or explanation, she would come up with another question or another subject, and I would again start talking. Now and then she would hush me:

"*Ssh!* Speak more softly!"

There were pauses too. Twice I thought she had dropped asleep, but her eyes, which had closed for an instant, immediately opened again with no sign of tiredness or fatigue, as if she had merely closed them in order to see more clearly. On one such occasion, I think she became aware of my rapt gaze, and she closed her eyes again, whether quickly or slowly I can't recall. Other memories of that night appear to me as truncated or confused. I contradict myself, stumble. One memory does still remain fresh, though; at one point, she, who I had only thought of as "nice-looking" before, looked really pretty, positively lovely. She was standing up, arms folded; out of politeness, I made as if to stand up, too, but she stopped me, placing one hand on my shoulder and obliging me to sit down again. I thought she was about to say something, but, instead, she shivered, as if she suddenly felt cold, then turned and sat in the chair where I had been sitting when she entered the room. From there, she glanced up at the mirror above the couch and commented on the two engravings on the wall.

"They're getting old, those pictures. I've already asked Chiquinho to buy some new ones."

Chiquinho was her husband. The pictures exemplified the man's main interest. One was a representation of Cleopatra, and I can't remember the other one, but both were of women. They were perhaps rather vulgar, but, at the time, I didn't think them particularly ugly.

"They're pretty," I said.

"Yes, but they're rather faded now. And frankly I would prefer two images of saints. These are more suited to a boy's bedroom or a barber's shop."

"A barber's shop? But you've never been in one, have you?"

"No, but I imagine that, while they're waiting, the customers talk about girls and love affairs and, naturally, the owner brightens up the place with a few pretty pictures. The ones over there just don't seem appropriate in a family home. At least, that's what I think, but then I often have strange thoughts. Anyway, I don't like them. In my prayer niche I have a really beautiful statuette of Our Lady of the Conception, my patron saint, but you can't hang a sculpture on the wall, much as I would like to."

This talk of prayer niches reminded me of mass, and it occurred to me that it might be getting late, and I was just about to mention this. I did, I think, get as far as opening my mouth, but immediately closed it again to listen to what she was saying, so gently, touchingly, softly, that my soul grew indolent and I forgot all about mass and church. She was talking about her devotions as a child and as a young girl. She then moved on to stories about dances, about outings she'd made, memories of Paquetá, all woven almost seamlessly together. When she grew tired of the past, she spoke about the present, about her household duties and the burdens of family life, which, before she married, she had been told were many, but which were not, in fact, burdensome at all. She didn't mention that she was twenty-seven when she married, but I knew that already.

She was no longer pacing up and down as she had been to begin with, but stayed almost frozen in the same pose. She no longer kept her large eyes fixed on me, but glanced around at the walls.

"This room needs repapering," she said after a while, as if talking to herself.

I agreed, simply in order to say something and to try to shake off that strange, magnetic sleep or whatever it was trammeling my tongue and my senses. I both wanted and didn't want to end that conversation; I made an effort to take my eyes off her, and I did so out of a sense of respect, but then, fearing that she might think I was bored, when I wasn't at all, I quickly brought my gaze back to her. The conversation was gradually dying. Out in the street, utter silence reigned.

We sat without speaking for some time, I don't know for how long. The only sound came from the study, the faint noise of a mouse gnawing away at something, and this did at last rouse me from my somnolent state; I tried to speak, but couldn't. Conceição appeared to be daydreaming. Then, suddenly, I heard someone banging on the window outside, and a voice shouting:

"Midnight mass! Midnight mass!"

"Ah, there's your friend," she said, getting up. "How funny! You were the one who was supposed to wake him up, but there he is waking you. Off you go. It must be time."

"Is it midnight already?" I asked.

"It must be."

"Midnight mass!" came the voice again, accompanied by more banging on the window.

"Quick, off you go. Don't keep him waiting. It was my fault. Good night. See you tomorrow."

And, with the same swaying gait, Conceição slipped silently back down the corridor. I went out into the street, where my neighbor was waiting. We set off to the church. More than once during mass, the figure of Conceição interposed itself between me and the priest, but let's put that down to my seventeen years. The following morning, over breakfast, I described the mass and the congregation, but Conceição showed not a flicker of interest. During the day, she was her usual natural, benign self and made no mention of our conversation the previous night. At New Year, I went home to Mangaratiba. By the time I returned to Rio in March, the notary had died of apoplexy. Conceição was living in Engenho Novo, but I neither visited her nor met her again. I later heard that she had married her late husband's articled clerk.

Christmas on the Ferry

Lygia Fagundes Telles

I don't want to, nor should I recall here why I found myself on that ferry. All I know is that all around was silence and darkness. And I felt at ease in that solitude. There were only four passengers on the crude, uncomfortable vessel. A lamp illuminated us with its faltering light: an old man, a woman with a child, and me.

The old man, a ragged drunk, had stretched out on the bench, addressed a few gentle words to an invisible neighbor, and was now sleeping. The woman was seated between us, holding the child wrapped in cloth tightly in her arms. She was young and pale. The long, dark cloak that covered her head made her look like an ancient figure.

I thought about speaking to her as soon as I boarded the boat. But we must have been already almost at the end of the trip and until that moment I hadn't addressed her. The idleness of conversation seemed incongruous on a boat so bare, so devoid of artifice. We were solitary. And still, it was better to do nothing, say nothing, just contemplate the black furrow the boat was tracing in the river.

I hunched over the railing of worm-eaten wood. Lit a cigarette. There we were, the four of us, as silent as the departed on an old ferry carrying the dead through the darkness. Yet, we were alive. And it was Christmas.

The box of matches slipped out of my hands and almost tumbled into the river. I squatted to pick it up. Then, feeling a few splashes on my face, I bent over until I could dip the tips of my fingers in the water.

—So cold—surprised, drying my hand.

—But in the morning, it's warm.

I turned to the woman, who was rocking the child and watching me with a half-smile. I sat down next to her on the bench. She had lovely light eyes, extraordinarily bright. I noticed that her clothes (poor, threadbare clothes) were full of character, imbued with a certain dignity.

—In the morning, this river is warm—she insisted, looking me in the eye.

—Warm?

—Warm and green, so green that the first time I washed a piece of clothing in it I thought it would come out green. Is this your first time in these parts?

I looked down at the floor of broad, worn planks. And responded with another question:

—Do you live nearby?

—In Lucena. I've taken this boat I don't know how many times before, but I didn't expect that today . . .

The child began to fuss, whimpering. The woman pressed it closer to her breast. She covered its head with a shawl and began to lull it to sleep with the gentle motion of a rocking chair. Her hands poked agitatedly through the black shawl, but her face was serene.

—Your child?

—Yes. He's sick, I'm going to see a specialist. The druggist in Lucena thought I should see a doctor *today*. Only yesterday he was well, but he suddenly took a turn for the worse. A fever, just a fever . . . But God won't abandon me.

—Is he the youngest?

She raised her head quickly. Her sharp chin was proud, but her gaze was gentle.

—He's the only one. My first died last year. He climbed the wall. He was playing magician, when suddenly he said, I'm going to fly! And he threw himself off. The fall wasn't long, the wall wasn't high, but he fell in such a way . . . He was just a little more than four years old.

I tossed my cigarette toward the river, but the butt hit the railing and came rolling back across the floor, still lit. I reached it with the toe of my shoe and slowly rubbed it out. I needed to turn the conversation to the child that was there, though sick. But alive.

—And this one? How old is he?

—He's about to turn one. —And, in a different tone, bending her head to her shoulder: —He was such a happy child. He was totally obsessed with magic. Obviously, nothing resulted, but it was very funny . . . His last trick was perfect, I'm going to fly! he said, opening his arms. And he flew.

I stood. I wanted to be alone in the night, without memories, without compassion. But ties (those human bonds) threatened to involve me. I had managed to avoid them until that moment. And now I didn't have the strength to break them.

—Is your husband waiting for you?

—My husband left me.

I sat down and felt like laughing. Unbelievable. It had been madness to ask the first question because now I couldn't stop, ah! that system of communicating vessels.

—Was it a long time ago? That your husband . . .

—It was about six months ago. We were doing so well, so very well. It was then that he met this old girlfriend by chance, he mentioned her, joking, Bila got uglier. You know that between the two of us it was me who ended up being more beautiful? I won't mention it again. One morning he got up like every morning, drank his coffee, read the paper, played with the boy, and went to work. Before he left he even did this with his hand, I was in the kitchen washing the dishes and he said goodbye through the wire screen of the door, I even remember that I wanted to open the door, I don't like seeing anyone talking to me with that mesh in the middle . . . But my hands were wet. I received the letter in the late afternoon. He sent a letter. I went to live with my mother in a house that we rented near my little school. I'm a teacher.

I gazed at the tumultuous clouds that flowed in the same direction as the river. Unbelievable. She continued to tell of successive misfortunes with such calm, in the tone of someone listing events without having actually taken part in them. As if the poverty evinced in her patched clothes wasn't enough, she had lost her little boy, her husband, and she saw a shadow looming over the second son cradled in her arms. And there she was without the slightest protest, trusting. Apathy? No, those ever so lively eyes, those energetic hands couldn't belong to someone apathetic. A certain irritation made me go on.

—You're resigned.

—I have faith, ma'am. God has never abandoned me.

—God—I repeated blankly.

—You don't believe in God?

—I do—I murmured. And on hearing the weak sound of my affirmative, without knowing why, I was embarrassed. I understood now. *There* was the secret of that certainty, that calm. It was that faith that can move mountains . . .

She shifted the child, passing him from her right shoulder to her left. And she began, with a voice hot with feeling:

—It was soon after the death of my son. I woke up one night in such despair that I went outside into the street, I put on a jacket and went out barefoot, crying like a madwoman, calling for him! I sat down on a bench in the garden where he'd play all afternoon. And I was begging, begging with such intensity that he, who so loved magic, would magically appear before me just one more time, he didn't have to stay, if he would show himself for just a moment, at least one more time, just once more! When I had no more tears left, I leaned my head on the bench, and I don't know how I fell asleep. And so, I dreamed, and in the dream, God appeared to me, I mean, I felt him take my hand in his hand of light. And I saw my son playing with the Baby Jesus in the Garden of Eden. As soon as he saw me, he stopped playing and came laughing to meet me and gave me many, many kisses . . . His joy was so great that I woke up laughing too, with the sun shining upon me.

I didn't know what to say. I sketched a quick gesture, and then, just to do something, I lifted the edge of the shawl that covered the child's head. I let the shawl fall again and turned toward the river. The boy was dead. I locked my hands together to control the tremor that shook me. He was dead. His mother continued to rock him, pressing him to her chest. But he was dead.

I leaned out over the railing of the boat and breathed with difficulty: it was as if I was submersed up to my chest in the water. I heard the woman stir behind me.

—We're arriving—she announced.

I quickly picked up my satchel. The important thing now was to escape, flee, before she made the discovery, run far from that horror. Slowing, the boat made a long turn before docking. The ticket seller appeared and began to shake the sleeping old man:

—We've arrived! . . . Hey! We've arrived!

I approached the woman, avoiding her gaze.

—I think we'd better say goodbye here.—I said quickly, holding out my hand.

She didn't seem to notice my gesture. She got up and made a movement as if to pick up her bag. I helped her, but instead of taking the bag I held out to her, before I could even stop her, she moved aside the shawl covering her baby's head.

—The little sleepyhead's woken up! And look here, it seems he doesn't have a fever at all anymore.

—He woke up?!

She smiled:

—Look . . .

I bent over. The child had opened his eyes—those eyes I had seen closed for good. And he yawned, rubbing his little hand on his flushed face. I stared, speechless.

—Well, Merry Christmas!—she said, pulling the bag over her arm.

Under the black cloak, the edges crossed and thrown back, her face shone. I shook her strong hand and followed her with my eyes until she disappeared into the night.

Led by the ticket seller, the old man passed me, resuming his affectionate dialogue with his invisible neighbor. I got off the boat last, still turning around twice to look at the river. And I could imagine how it would be in the early morning: warm and green. Warm and green.

Christmas

Olavo Bilac

In the wilderness, a hymn from the stable in dark night:
The wind that filled the sky with hopeful omen . . .
The trees: "Thou wilt be the dew and sun!"
All arms: "Glory will be thine!" "Fate wilt Thou best!" sang the moonlight.

And the bread: "Thou wilt the bread of Earth and Heaven bestow!"
And the water: "Thou wilt relieve the martyr and the thirsty!"
And the straw: "Thou wilt bend the necks of the lofty!"
And the roof: "Thou wilt raise from shame the low."

And the kings: "King, under palms wilt Thou enter the kingdom Thine!"
And the shepherds: "Shepherd, Thou wilt the elect call!"
And the star: "Like God, upon all souls wilt Thou shine!"

Mute and humble, though, was Mary, like a slave,
Her eyes looked earthward, in weeping all undone:
Being poor, she was afeared; being a mother, tears she gave.

Snowstorm

Bruna Dantas Lobato

Snow started to leave a tinge of lifelessness on everything, and I stopped going outside, stayed indoors as much as I could, in layers of fleece. Everyone left the campus for warmer places for the break, and I stayed there, in the dorm that looked like a milk carton, with its modern shape and single gable, never went anywhere too far from it.

In the afternoons, I worked at the campus mailroom, where I watched the stacks of letters grow, unopened. I put slim envelopes in their slots. I sorted Amazon deliveries, media mail, care packages in padded envelopes sent Priority from loving parents. Dubrowsky, Dunn, Dunton.

There was intimacy in watching the movements of the campus, the coming and going, even in everyone's absence.

Then, in the evenings, I went back to my room and read until I ran out of pages. Then I called my mom on Skype.

And have you been eating? she asked. Have you been going outside? Being careful out there? Washing your undies in the shower, like I taught you?

She worried about me all alone on campus. She worried about me in the dead of winter. She worried about me living so far away, alone in America.

She'd watched a movie about a couple of girls left behind at a boarding school upstate. The snow made the campus look bleak. Emma Roberts had dark circles under her eyes. Everyone died.

Don't go down into the basement, she said. Avoid long hallways. Don't go out late at night.

When she heard on the news that a snowstorm was passing through Vermont, she e-mailed me to ask if I needed company. A friend to marvel at the thunder with, she wrote.

I called her as soon as I woke up, before I ate my breakfast.

I've never seen a snowstorm, she said. She brought her face closer to the screen. Where is it?

It's over, I said.

I showed her my window. The sky looked blank like a sheet, icicles hanging from the frame like teeth in a child's drawing. Sunlight flooded the Webcam, and for a moment my corner of the screen was all white. I reappeared as a silhouette, and then as my full self again.

Call me if something happens, while it's still happening, she said. I want to see it live.

Then she went on to list every storm fact she knew.

Sandstorms on Mars, other storms on the moon. Every tragedy on Earth. Floods, tsunamis, earthquakes. She talked until I had to say, Mom, it's getting late. I have to get ready for work.

On a particularly cold day, I sent my mother a picture of the snow falling onto the soccer field out my window, which I knew she found serene, beautiful even, but this time she found it scary.

Does walking outside feel like being buried alive? she asked.

And I said that it didn't, though the truth was that sometimes it did. I'd have to dust the snow off my shoulders and the creases in my coat before I walked in, my legs heavy, my jaw frozen, my hands burning.

She told me to stay indoors as much as I could, not to leave my room again until it was warm outside.

Then she shook her head.

No, don't listen to me.

She yawned then looked past me, at something behind her screen. A lock of her hair fell on her eyes, and she didn't move it away.

It was later there than where I was, way past midnight. I let her go to bed, and I stayed up, all the lights in my room still on.

I sat in front of the computer, wondering what I should do next, now that I was alone. The Victorian novels I had to read for the upcoming semester sat unopened on my desk. I felt it would take too much effort to enter their world that night, to move between Brazil and the United States and then England in the course of a day.

The computer screen went dark, and I saw my own face reflected in it. I looked pale and tired, papery, even, as if covered in mildew. I got up and splashed cold water on my face in the bathroom down the hall, then put on my coat and boots and went out on a walk.

From the middle of the soccer field, in the dark, I could see into my bedroom on the third floor, and into the bedrooms of my neighbors. A shadow moved across a room. Two girls laughed together in another, tilting back their heads, with no sound. In my room, the window framed a perfect image of stillness. The whole world seemed to quieten down for that moment, for me to look at what my life looks like.

I called her again when I thought she'd be awake, and her face glowed in the dark, lit up by nothing but the computer screen.

Were you asleep?

The light was giving me a headache, she said, and took her hand to her brow.

Everything gave her migraines in those days. She felt dizzy, her ears rang, her eyes twitched. To protect herself, she had to live in a world of blandness, often in silence, often in the dark, warm gauze over her eyes.

It occurred to me that she'd love the milk carton and the campus. The carpeted halls and the snow muffling every sound, the dining-hall food, the constant darkness, nighttime always spilling into mornings.

I told her this, and she said, Can you imagine? If the moment I got there and ate your food and slept on your bed and walked around in your clothes I was suddenly cured?

I told her about my walk to the soccer field.

She smiled and said, So it turns out you do listen to what I say.

I do, I do.

Just don't go on these walks when it's dark out, she said. Have you heard about the Filipino student who got murdered somewhere in New York last week? Not too far from you.

I laughed, happy that she was back to being so unmistakably herself.

When winter break was almost over, my mother e-mailed me to say that she'd received the package I'd sent her for Christmas, a few weeks too late, when I'd already forgotten about it.

On Skype, she waited with the box on her lap so we could open it together, her hands on my address.

I can't believe this came all the way from America, she said.

She turned the box to the screen to show me the customs label I'd filled out.

Look, I'm touching your handwriting, she said. Might as well be touching your hand.

She cut the tape open with her kitchen shears and found the card I'd written for her, a brown dog running down a snowy hill.

Read it to me, I said.

Querida mãe, she said. Feliz Natal.

But then she couldn't make out what the rest of it said.

Your handwriting has changed, she said. I can barely recognize it.

I don't write in cursive anymore, I said. Not since I was a kid.

That's it, she said. It's very grownup now. I no longer see my little girl in it.

Show it to me and I'll read it.

She placed the open card in front of the camera and I tried to make sense of what I'd written, but all I saw was a blur. Neat lines of blur.

She went through the rest of the contents of the box: a tiny bottle of maple syrup, a little bag of peppermint candy, a blue shawl.

She put the computer on the coffee table then stood up and draped the shawl over her shoulders, swaying from side to side.

It's like a hug, she said. A cocoon.

She sat back down and curled up on the couch, covering the length of her body with it, the shawl as a blanket, all the way up to her chin.

Will you talk me to sleep?

I nodded, but then I couldn't think of anything to say.

I thought maybe I could read her a story instead. Something soothing, nothing like the news.

I looked around my room for a book in Portuguese, something we could both understand, and then I realized there was nothing. All the books around me were in English, and every flyer, magazine, brochure. Even my own diaries.

Read in English, then, she said. I don't mind. I just want to hear your voice.

She closed her eyes and waited, stroking the tassels at the edge of the shawl.

I grabbed one of the Victorian novels I'd been studying and opened it to a random page. I told her all it said about orphans, and fortunes, and fate.

I read for what felt like an hour. Twenty-eight pages' worth of story.

Sometimes she nodded, until she didn't, her lids shut, her head heavy over one shoulder.

And then what? Was I supposed to hang up on her, on my own mother?

I muted my mike and kept watch for most of the night. Her occasional stirs, her face glowing in the dark, her hair over her eyes. The restlessness of her sleep.

Feast Day

Graciliano Ramos

Fabiano, Vitória, and the boys were going to the Christmas celebrations in town. It was three in the afternoon and exceedingly hot; small whirlwinds spread clouds of dust and dry leaves over the yellowed trees.

They had closed up the house, crossed the yard, gone down the slope, and were stumbling along on the stones, like sore-hoofed oxen. Fabiano, cramped in the suit of duck old Miss Terta had sewed for him, wearing a baize hat, a collar and tie, and thin-leather gaiters, tried to hold himself straight, something he did not ordinarily do. Vitória, clad in her red, flowered dress, had a hard time keeping her balance in her high-heeled shoes. She insisted on wearing the kind city girls did, and she stumbled as she went along. The boys were wearing jackets and trousers for the first time. At home they wore just a little shirt of stripped cotton or else went naked. Fabiano, however, had bought ten ells of white cloth at the store and had charged old Miss Terta with making suits for him and his boys. Old Miss Terta had said the cloth was hardly enough, but Fabiano had paid no attention, sure she only intended to steal the scraps. As a result the suits were short and tight, and showed much patching.

Fabiano tried to overlook these disadvantages. He walked along stiffly, his belly sticking out and his shoulders thrown back, gazing at the distant range of hills. Normally he looked at the ground, so as to avoid stones, stumps, holes, and snakes. The forced posture wearied him. When he got to the sand of the riverbed he realized he could never go the three leagues to town that way. He pulled off his gaiters, stuffed his socks in his pocket, took off his coat, collar, and necktie, and heaved a sigh of relief. Vitória decided to follow his example. She took off her shoes and stockings, tying them up in her kerchief. The children put their sandals under their arms and felt quite at ease.

The dog, who had been tagging along behind, joined the group at this point. If she had appeared sooner, in all probability Fabiano would have chased her back and she would have spent the holiday with the goats that dirtied the shed with their droppings. With his collar and tie rumpled in his pocket, his coat over his shoulder, and his gaiters on the end of a stick, the herdsman felt closer to her and accepted her company.

He resumed his normal stance, walking with a sway, his head bent forward. Vitória, the two boys, and the dog accompanied him. The afternoon went by rapidly, and by nightfall they were at the creek bank where the street began.

There Fabiano stopped, sat down, and washed his horny feet, striving to get the dirt out of their deep cracks. Without drying, he tried to put his gaiters and socks on. It was a struggle: the heels of the cotton socks got balled up on his instep and the thin-leather gaiters resisted like shy virgins. Vitória pulled up her skirt, sat down on the ground, and likewise washed. The two boys waded into the brook, where they scrubbed their feet, then got out, put on their sandals, and stood watching their parents' movements. Vitória finished and got up, but Fabiano was puffing with exasperation. He had overcome the obstinacy of one of those cursed gaiters, but the other was stuck and all his tugs on the straps were in vain.

Vitória offered suggestions which only served to irritate her husband. There was no way of getting his heel down where it belonged. A harder pull on the strap at the back caused it to break off in his hand. Fabiano energetically grasped at the elastic instead, but to no avail. He got up, resolved to start down the street like that, limping, with one leg longer than the other. In rage, mingled with hope, he gave a violent stamp on the ground. His flesh squeezed, his bones cracked, his damp sock tore, and his cramped foot slipped into place in its leather prison. Fabiano heaved a long sigh of relief and pain. Then he tried to fasten his hard collar around his neck, but his trembling fingers weren't equal to the task. Vitória came to his aid; the collar button slipped into its little hole and the tie was knotted. Their dirty, sweaty hands left black marks on the collar.

"It's all right now," grunted Fabiano.

They crossed the plank bridge and started down the street. Vitória stumbled as she walked, because of her high heels, and held her umbrella, handle down, ferrule up, wrapped in her kerchief. It would be impossible to say why she carried it handle down. She herself could not have explained it. She had always seen other country women do thus and she had adopted the custom.

Fabiano marched along stiffly.

The two boys stared at the streetlamps and divined wonders. They were afraid, rather than curious, and consequently walked softly, lest they attract other people's attention. They had always supposed there were worlds different from that of the ranch, marvelous worlds in the blue hills. This, however, was peculiar. How could there be so many houses and so many people? Surely the men were going to have a fight. Would these people be hostile and forbid them to go in among the stands? They were used to having their ears pulled and their heads cracked. Perhaps the strangers wouldn't whack them as Vitória did, but the youngsters shrank back, clung to the walls, half-dazzled, their ears full of strange sounds.

They arrived at the church and went in. The dog stayed trotting around on the sidewalk, looking at the street with distrust. In her opinion everything ought to be dark, because it was night, and the people walking in the square should go to bed. Raising her muzzle, she noted an odor that made her want to cough. They were making entirely too much noise around there and the light was too bright, but what really bothered her was that smell of smoke.

The boys too were astonished. In their suddenly expanded world Fabiano and Vitória loomed up much less impressively: they were smaller than the figures on the altars. The boys didn't know what altars were, but they gathered that the objects on them must be precious. The lights and the singing enchanted them. The only light on the ranch was that of the kitchen fire and the kerosene lamp that hung by its handle from a peg in the wall; the only singing consisted of Vitória's blessing and Fabiano's halloos. The halloo was sad sounding, a monotonous, wordless tune that lulled the cattle.

Fabiano remained staring at the images and the lighted candles in silence. He was uncomfortable in his new suit; he held his neck stretched and walked as if on coals. The crowd cramped and hampered him more than his suit. When he had his chaps, jacket, and chest protector on, he was boxed in like an armadillo in its shell, but he could leap on the back of an animal and go flying off across the brushland. Now he couldn't even turn around; hands and arms brushed against his body. He remembered the beating he had taken and the night he had spent in jail. The feeling he now had wasn't very different from that which he had experienced as a prisoner. It was as if the hands and arms of the crowd were trying to grab hold of him, subdue him, and press him into a corner. He looked at the faces around him. Obviously the people who had gathered there didn't notice him, but Fabiano felt as if he were surrounded by enemies; he feared he might get into arguments and that the night might end badly. He puffed and tried uselessly to fan himself with his hat. It was difficult to move; he was practically tied. Slowly he managed to make his way through the throng, slipping over to the holy-water font, where he stopped, fearful of losing sight of his wife and sons. He stood on tiptoe but this only brought a groan from him: his blistered heels were beginning to hurt. He made out the bun of Vitória's hair. She was more or less hidden by a pillar. Probably the boys were with her. The church got fuller and fuller. To make out his wife's head, Fabiano had to stretch and turn his own. And his collar was digging into his neck. The gaiters and the collar were indispensable. He couldn't go to the novena wearing sandals and a cotton shirt, open in the front, exposing his hairy chest. That would be a lack of respect. Since he had religion he went to church once a year, and as long as he could remember he had seen people dress like this on feast days, in starched trousers and jacket, gaiters, baize hat, collar, and necktie. He would not risk breaking tradition, even if he suffered for it. He thought he was performing a duty. He tried to straighten up, but his will flagged. His spine sagged naturally, and his arms dangled awkwardly.

Comparing himself with the city folk, Fabiano held himself inferior. This was why he was afraid the others would make fun of him. He assumed a surly expression and avoided conversations. People talked to him only to get something out of him. The tradesmen cheated on measure, price, and accounts. The boss's figuring with pen and ink he could not understand; the last time he met with him there had been some confusion about numbers, and Fabiano, his brain awhirl, had left the office in indignation, sure he had been cheated. He took a beating from all of them. The clerks, the tradesmen, and the landowner stole the shirt off his back, and those who had no dealings with him laughed when they saw him go stumbling down the street. This was why Fabiano tried to avoid these people. He knew his new suit, cut and sewed by old Miss Terta, his collar, his tie, his gaiters, and his baize hat made him look ridiculous, but he didn't want to think about that.

"Lazy, thieving, gossiping, good-for-nothings!"

He was convinced that all the town folk were evil. He bit his lips. He couldn't afford to say anything like that. For a much lesser offence he had been whacked with a knife and had had to sleep in jail. Now that policeman in khaki– He shook his head to get rid of the unpleasant recollection and sought for a friendly face in the crowd. If he found someone he knew, he would call him out on the sidewalk, embrace him, smile, and clap his hands. Then they would talk about cattle. He shivered and tried to make out the bun of Vitória's hair. He had to be careful not to get too far from his wife and children. He moved in their direction and came up to them at the moment that the church was beginning to empty.

Pushing and shoving they made their way out and down the steps. Bumped and jostled, Fabiano again thought of the policeman in khaki. Out in the square, on passing by the courbaril tree he turned his face away. For no reason at all the wretch had gone and provoked him, stepping on his foot. He had turned away, politely. But since the other fellow had persisted, he had lost his patience and had flown off the handle. The result: he had been whacked on the back with a knife and had spent a night in jail.

He invited his wife and the boys to take a ride on the merry-go-round, saw them seated, and amused himself for a while watching them ride by. Then he went to the gambling booths. He scratched, pulled out his handkerchief, untied it and counted his money, tempted to risk it on a game of dice. If he were lucky he could buy the bed of untanned leather his wife dreamed of. He went and had a drink of rum at one of the stands, came back, and circled around in indecision, looking at Vitória in a mute appeal for her opinion. She made a gesture of disapproval and Fabiano withdrew, remembering the game at Inácio's with the policeman in khaki. He had been cheated; he was sure he had been cheated. He went back to the stand and had another drink of rum. Little by little he lost his inhibitions.

"Feast days a fellow has to celebrate," he declared.

He had still one more drink; then, straightening up, he stared at the passers-by in defiance. He was resolved to do something crazy. If he came on the policeman in khaki there would be a real row. He walked around among the stands, swaggering, kicking at the ground, oblivious of the blisters on his feet. He was looking for trouble: he wanted to show that good-for-nothing! He paid no attention to his wife and sons, who were following him.

"I'd like to see a real man!" he bawled.

In the hubbub of the square no one heard the challenge, and Fabiano withdrew behind the stands, to the other side of the vendors of sweetmeats. He was in a mean mood but not entirely without a sense of prudence. There back of the stands he could give vent to wrath and spout threats and insults at invisible enemies. Driven by opposing forces, he took certain precautions in exposing himself. He knew that an outburst was dangerous; he was afraid the policeman in khaki might appear suddenly and tramp on his foot with his boot. The policeman was a paltry fellow, but he acted brave in the company of his companions. It was a good idea to avoid him. The thought of him at times was unbearable though, and Fabiano was getting even. Stimulated by the rum he had drunk, he grew bold.

"Where is that bully? I'd like to see a fellow with nerve enough to say I'm ugly! Aren't there any real men around here?"

He stammered out his challenge with a vague fear of being heard. No one appeared. Fabiano blustered and shouted they were all lily-livered cowards. Yes they were! After a lot of yelling, supposing there were men there, hiding from fear of him, he insulted them,

"Pack of–"

He stopped in an agony of cold sweat, his mouth full of saliva, unable to find the right word. A pack of what? He had the word on the tip of his tongue, but that tongue was swollen and stiff. Fabiano spat and fixed glassy eyes on his wife and boys. He drew back a few steps, with a feeling of nausea. Then he again approached the area of bright lights, limping, and went and sat down on the sidewalk in front of a store. He felt limp and dispirited; his enthusiasm had chilled. A pack of what? He repeated his question, without knowing what he was seeking. He looked closely at his wife's face but couldn't make out her features. Could Vitória be aware of his fluster? There were other back-country men there talking, and Fabiano found them disgusting. If he didn't feel so qualmish, belching and sweating, he would get into a fight with them. His mind, already befuddled by the question that was troubling him, was further bothered by the thought that those people had no right to sit on the sidewalk. He wanted them to leave him alone with his wife, his boys, and the dog. A pack of what? He gave a harsh cry and slapped his hands together.

"A pack of dogs!"

Having discovered the expression that had so stubbornly eluded him, he was elated. A pack of dogs. Obviously, back-country people like him were no better than dogs. He reached with his hands for his wife and boys and found they were seated beside him. A violent cramp in his neck made his face twist in pain and his mouth again filled with saliva. He started to spit. Calmer, he breathed deeply and wiped a thread of saliva from his chin with his fingers. He was dizzy, and had an annoying buzzing in his ears. He was going to swear that he had been in danger and had shown courage, but at the same time he felt he had done wrong.

Now he was sluggish and drowsy. While he had been showing off, with a head full of rum, he had paid no attention to the blisters on his feet. Now that he had calmed down, the gaiters hurt entirely too much. He pulled them off, took off his socks, got rid of his collar, tie, and coat, which he rolled up into a pillow, and, stretching out on the sidewalk, he pulled his baize hat over his eyes and went to sleep with a queasy stomach.

Vitória was in difficulties; there was a certain necessary matter she needed urgently to attend to and she didn't know how to go about it. She might seek concealment at the other side of the square, behind the stands and the stools on which the vendors of sweetmeats sat. She arose, her mind half made up, then squatted down again. Could she leave the boys with her husband in that state? She restrained herself, looking desperately in every direction, for her need was great. She slipped away unobtrusively and came to the corner of the store, where a crowd of women were squatting. And, staring at the house fronts and the paper lanterns, she wet the ground and the feet of the other country women. She made her way slowly back to her family, took from her pocket her clay pipe, packed and lit it, and gave long puffs of satisfaction. Having relieved herself, she looked with interest at the people swarming in the square, the auction table, and the bright trails of the rockets. Really, life wasn't too bad. She gave a shiver as she thought of the drought, of the terrible trek they had made under the burning sun, seeing nothing but bones and twisted branches. She wiped the recollection from her mind, turning to the beautiful things there at hand. The noise of the crowd was pleasant to hear; the drone of the hurdy-gurdy at the merry-go-round never ceased. All Vitória needed for life to be good was a bed like Tomás the miller's. She sighed, thinking of the bed of tree branches on which they slept, and squatted there smoking, her eyes and ears wide open so as to lose nothing of the festivities.

The boys exchanged impressions in a whisper, worried at the disappearance of the dog. They tugged at their mother's sleeve. What could have happened to the dog? Vitória raised her arm in a vague gesture and pointed in a couple of directions with the stem of her pipe. The boys persisted in their questioning.

Where could the dog be? Indifferent to the church, the paper lanterns, the stands with things for sale, the gaming tables, and the rockets, they concentrated solely on the legs of the passersby. Poor thing, she must be lost among them, getting kicked by all those feet.

Suddenly the dog appeared. She jumped up on the sidewalk, dived through the women›s skirts, climbed over Fabiano, and came up to her friends, her tongue and tail manifesting a lively contentment. The older boy grabbed her. She was safe! They tried to make her understand that they had been greatly worried about her, but she paid no attention to their explanation. She just thought they were wasting time in a funny place full of strange odors. She felt like barking in opposition to all this, but realizing that she wouldn't win anyone to her way of thinking she dropped her tail and curled up, resigned to the caprices of her masters.

The boys were of an opinion similar to hers. Looking at the stores, the stands, and the auction table, they conferred together in amazement. They had accepted the fact that there were a lot of people in the world, and now they busied themselves with the discovery of a huge number of things. They discussed in a whisper the surprises with which they were filled. It was impossible to imagine so many marvelous things all at one time. The younger boy timidly expressed a doubt to his brother: Could all that have been made by people? The older boy hesitated. He looked at the stores, at the stands with their lights, and at the girls in their pretty dresses. He shrugged his shoulders. Perhaps it had all been made by people. Then a new problem presented itself to his mind and he whispered it in his brother's ear: In all probability those things had names. The younger boy looked at him questioningly. Yes, surely all the precious things exhibited on the altars and on the shelves in the stores had names.

They began to discuss the perplexing question. How could men keep so many words in their heads? It was impossible; no one could have so vast a store of knowledge. Free of names, things seemed distant and mysterious. They had not been made by people and it was imprudent for people to meddle with them. Seen from afar they were pretty. Filled with admiration and awe the boys talked in low voices so as not to unleash the strange forces the things might contain.

The dog was drowsing. From time to time she shook her head and wrinkled her muzzle. The city was full of smells of sweat which she found disconcertingly unfamiliar.

Vitoria seemed to see amid the stands the bed of Tomas the miller—a real, honest-to-goodness bed.

Fabiano, lying on his back, snored, the brim of his hat covering his eyes, his head resting on his thin-leather gaiters. He was having a nightmare, and the dog noted that he gave off a smell which rendered him unrecognizable. Fabiano tossed and made noises. Many policemen in khaki had appeared and were trampling on his feet with enormous military boots, threatening him with terrible knives.

A Christmas Miracle

Lima Barreto

The Andaraí district is very melancholy and very damp. The mountains that adorn our city are even higher out there and are still covered by the dense vegetation that must have been even more abundant in bygone days. And the dark gray of the trees seems to turn the horizon almost black and the district even sadder.

When the mountain range overlooks the sea, it breaks the monotony of the scene: the sunlight gushes forth more freely and the little, mundane things of humankind acquire a brightness and cheeriness that has more to do with perception than reality. And that applies to both the humble houses in Botafogo and the bombastic "mansions" in Copacabana; but further inland, in Andaraí, everything is overwhelmed by the mountains and their gloomy vegetation.

It was in that district that Feliciano Campossolo Nunes lived. He was deputy director of the National Treasury. The house was his own and, on at the front cornice, its grandiose name was displayed: Villa Sebastiana. I won't bore you with how tasteful its façade was, and how elegant its proportions. At the front there was a small garden that extended, on the left, about a meter beyond the façade, which was the width of the side veranda that almost encircled the house. Campossolo was a stern, bald man, with a goatee, a large belly, fleshy hands, and short fingers. He never let his Morocco-leather attaché case, in which he brought home the office papers with the intention of not reading them, out of his sight. When out and about he'd also usually be seen carrying an umbrella with a gold knob and silk lining. Overweight, and with short legs, he had great difficulty, burdened as he was with those items, in climbing the two steps of the trams run by the Rio de Janeiro Tramway, Light & Power Company.

Oh! And he wore a bowler hat.

He lived in Villa Sebastiana with his wife and their only child, Mariazinha, a young woman who was not yet married.

His wife, Dona Sebastiana, after whom their house was named and with whose money it had been built, was taller than him, but there was nothing distinctive about her face other than an artificial addition: a small, gold-framed pince-nez that was secured behind one ear by a silk ribbon. She hadn't been born with that adornment, but might as well have been, as no one had ever seen her without it. Day or night, it was always firmly fixed on her nose. And when she wanted to have a really good look at someone or something, she'd lift her head and tilt it backward, with all the severity of a judge.

She was from the state of Bahia, as was her husband, but the only thing she had against Rio was the difficulty of obtaining seasonings for the moquecas, carurus and other Bahian dishes that she cooked so expertly, with the help of her black servant Inácia, who'd come with them from Salvador when Feliciano was transferred to Rio. If someone offered, she'd send them to look for some; and when she did manage to get them and to cook a really tasty moqueca, she'd completely forget that she was so far away from her beloved city of Tomé de Sousa.

Unlike her mother, Mariazinha had more or less forgotten that she was born there, and she'd become a proper Carioca. She was twenty years old, slim, shapely, taller than her father and about the same height as her mother. And she was pretty and completely without airs and graces. Her most beautiful feature was her eyes, which were pale gray flecked with black. But, as I say, she had no fashionable conceits, unlike most other girls.

So, these were the residents at Villa Sebastiana, that is, apart from a little black boy, but never the same one: every two months or so, for whatever reason, one would be replaced by another, the only difference being that the next one might be a bit paler or a bit darker.

On certain Sundays, Senhor Campossolo would invite some of his subordinates to lunch or dinner. But he was particular about which subordinates he invited. After all, he had an unmarried daughter and he couldn't let just any young man into his house, even if he happened to work at the National Treasury.

The ones he invited most frequently were his right-hand men in the section, the third-tier clerks Fortunato Guaicuru and Simplício Fontes. Fortunato had a law degree and was, more or less, Feliciano's secretary and his adviser on difficult matters; and Simplício was chief of protocol in the section, a position of great responsibility, because it required him to ensure that processes were followed to the letter and that the section was not open to accusations of laxity or negligence. So, these two were the most frequent guests at those delightful family gatherings. And Feliciano was mindful that he needed to find a husband for his daughter . . .

You're probably aware that parents normally try to marry off their daughters to someone of the same class as themselves: fathers who are businessmen seek out businessmen or clerks; military men, other military men; doctors, other doctors and so on. It's no surprise then that Section Head Campossolo should be looking out for a promising civil servant, and not just any civil servant, but a civil servant from his own department and, indeed, his own section.

Guaicuru was from Mato Grosso. His features were decidedly native Indian: prominent cheekbones, a short face, a big, hard chin, a moustache like wild boar bristles, receding forehead, and slightly bowed legs. He'd originally been appointed to the customs house in Corumbá before being transferred to the Goiás tax office, where he'd spent three or four years, earning a law degree in the process—because there's not a city in Brazil, whether it's the state capital or not, that doesn't have a law school. Once he'd got his degree, and the title of Doctor that went with it, he'd been promoted to the Mint and thence to the National Treasury. He never forgot to wear the ruby ring that marked him out as the holder of a law degree. He was a stout lad, with broad, straight shoulders, unlike Simplício, who was pale and weedy, with big black eyes and the look of a shrinking violet.

Simplício was from Rio and had achieved his post almost completely without the intervention of powerful backers. I wouldn't say he was more learned, but he was much better educated than Guaicuru. Yet he didn't have the latter's panache that, though it didn't win out over education in Mariazinha's heart, did in her mother's mind as regards finding a husband for her daughter. So Dona Sebastiana's attention, at the table, was directed almost solely to Guaicuru, who she'd arranged to sit opposite her, beside her daughter.

"Why don't you become a lawyer?" she asked. smiling, looking from him to her daughter with her haughty, four-eyed gaze.

"Because I don't have the time for it, Senhora . . . "

"What do you mean, you don't have the time for it? Felicianinho would agree to it, wouldn't you, Felicianinho?"

"But of course. I'm always happy to help my colleagues progress," said Campossolo, gravely.

Simplício, who was sitting to the left of Dona Sebastiana, was looking distractedly at the fruit basket and said nothing. Guaicuru was trying to think of something to say, other than the truth, which was that the law school he'd attended wasn't recognized.

"My colleagues might resent my leaving," was what he managed eventually.

But Dona Sebastiana only pressed on more forcibly:

"Nonsense! You wouldn't complain, would you Senhor Simplício?"

Hearing his name, the poor lad raised his eyes hurriedly from the fruit bowl and asked in trepidation:

"I beg your pardon, Dona Sebastiana?"

"Would you complain if Felicianinho allowed Guaicuru to leave the office to get a job as a lawyer?

"No."

And his eyes drifted back to the fruit bowl, alighting briefly on the beautiful eyes of Mariazinha. Campossolo kept on eating, and Dona Sebastiana continued:

"If I were you, I'd become a lawyer."

"I can't. It's not just the office that takes up my time. I'm writing a very large book."

Everyone looked up in surprise. Mariazinha glanced at Guaicuru; Dona Sebastiana tilted her pince-nezed face even further back; Simplício—who'd been looking at the painting of the dead game bird hanging by its legs that you see in the homes of so many bourgeois families hung alongside The Last Supper—Simplício, as I was saying, stared resolutely at his colleague, and Campossolo asked:

"What's it about?"

"Brazilian administrative law."

"It must be quite a work," observed Campossolo.

"I hope so."

Simplício continued to stare at Guaicuru as if he couldn't believe his ears. Noticing this, Guaicuru hastened to add:

"Would you like to hear what I'm proposing?"

All of them, except Mariazinha, replied almost in unison:

"Oh, yes! We would."

The graduate from Goiás straightened up in his chair and began:

"I'm connecting our Brazilian Administrative Law to the ancient Portuguese Administrative Law. Many people think there was no Administrative Law under the old regime, but there was. I'm going to study the mechanism of the state at that time, in so far as Portugal is concerned. And I'm going to consider the functions of the ministers and their subordinates through the lens of those old orders, regulations and royal decrees, and I'll show how the whole thing worked; and then I'll show how that rather moribund Public Law was transformed by the influx of liberal ideas; and how, having been transported to Brazil with the arrival here of Dom João VI, it was adapted to our context and was further modified by the ideas of the Revolution."

Hearing all this, Simplício couldn't help thinking, "Who taught him all that?"

But Guaicuru hadn't finished:

"It won't be a dry enumeration of dates or a transcription of decrees, orders-in-council etc. It will be something completely new. Something vibrant."

He broke off here, and Campossolo repeated, but even more gravely:

"It must be quite a work."

"And I've already got an editor!"

"Who's that?" asked Simplício.

"It's Jacinto. You know, I'm always going there to get legal books."

"Oh, yes!" said Simplício, trying not to smile. "It's the law bookshop."

"And when do you intend to have your work published, Doctor?" asked Dona Sebastiana.

"I'd like it to be before Christmas, in time for the pre-Christmas round of promotions, but . . . "

"Are there promotions before Christmas, Felicianinho?"

Senhora Sebastiana's husband replied:

"I believe so. The Cabinet have already requested recommendations and I've already given mine to the director."

"You should have told me!" said his wife, sounding put-out.

"We don't talk about things like that with our wives; they're state secrets," her husband proclaimed.

This business of the pre-Christmas promotions had introduced a rather depressing note to the meal. So, trying to reanimate the conversation, Dona Sebastiana turned once more to her husband:

"I wouldn't want you to tell me their names, but if it so happened that Dr Fortunato was to be promoted or . . . or our Simplício here, it would be good if I knew if a celebration was in order."

This didn't have the desired effect. The dejection deepened and, by the time coffee was served, there was almost complete silence.

When they stood up to leave the table, they all had a rather somber look, except for the kind Mariazinha, who tried to get the conversation going again. In the living room, before taking his leave, Simplício got the opportunity for two more, furtive, exchanges with the beguiling eyes of the young lady, who was smiling as if nothing were amiss. His colleague Fortunato stayed on, but everything felt so awkward that, before long, he too took his leave.

On the tram, there were just two things in Simplício's mind: Christmas and Guaicuru's law book. As to the latter, he was still thinking, "Where on earth did he learn all that? Guaicuru hardly knows anything!" And his thoughts about Christmas were, "If only our dear Lord Jesus . . . "

When the promotions were finally announced, it was Simplício who was promoted, because he'd been in the office much longer than Guaicuru. This particular minister took no notice of lobbying or of so-called law degrees from Goiás.

No-one was overlooked. But Guaicuru, who was working on a book that had already been written, was inwardly furious.

Dona Sebastiana's Christmas meal was in the northern style. At the dinner hour, Guaicuru, as was his habit, went to sit beside Mariazinha, but Dona Sebastiana had already raised her pince-nezed head.

"Come and sit beside me, Doctor. Our Simplício is going to sit over there."

They were married within the year and, even now, after the first flush of passion, they still are.

He maintained it was Our Lord Jesus Christ who married them. She maintained it was the promotion. But whether it was the one or the other, or the two together, it's a fact that they did get married. Guaicuru's book, however, has not yet been published . . .

It's Christmas Eve and I'm All Alone

Rubem Braga

It's Christmas Eve and I'm alone at home of a friend, who left for the farm. I might go out later. But I find myself easing into being alone, pleasantly melancholic in the quiet and comfortable house. I make a few phone calls, send friends long-distance hugs.

The few voices of men and women that respond, cheerfully, to mine—"Merry Christmas, happy holidays!"—are warm and do me good. We say these simple things with affection; we say them, and I think we mean them; and since we mean them, we deserve them. Merry Christmas!

I unwrap the bottle that a friend thought to send yesterday; I go inside, open the fridge, prepare a whisky, and go sit in the little garden, by the damp vegetation. I feel good, indulging myself in this glass, in this silent house, on this evening with its quiet streets. The garden has the sensible and unspoiled appeal of the woman who planted it. A small, leafy nook with colorful flowers, it seems to breathe and has the mysterious life of distant woods, an air of the countryside, a rather rustic happiness of greens, reds and yellows.

I think back, without resentment or nostalgia, on the year gone by. There's a painful shadow over it; I recall it, now that I'm alone, with a sort of reverence. There is also, deep in the dark and disordered landscape of this year, a bright patch of sunshine. I silently drink to these images of death and of life; within me, they are sisters. I think of other people. I feel a great tenderness for them; I'm a man alone, on a quiet night, next to some damp vegetation, drinking somberly in honor of a great many people.

Suddenly a car starts honking, loud, by my front gate. Maybe it's a friend come to wish me Merry Christmas or invite me out somewhere. I hesitate for a moment; no one can possibly think I'm home at this hour. But the horn is insistent. I get up with a certain excitement, look out at the street, and smile: it's the trash truck. It's so overloaded that it won't shut; so overloaded that it's as if it's carrying all the trash from the past year, all the trash from this life that we keep on living. Some Christmas gift!

The driver honks another couple of times, looking up at the window of a neighboring townhouse. I remember seeing at that widow a young black woman dressed in red, always humming and peering out over the street. She's definitely the one the idling driver is looking for, but the window remains dark and closed. Violently, he shifts his dark, dirty truck into gear, and drives off with a rumble, rattling the street.

I return to my tranquility, and to my whisky. But the frustration of the trash collector, and my own, have broken the solitary spell of this Christmas Eve. I close up the house and head out slowly, to humbly cadge a slice of ham and happiness at the home of some friends.

The Nativity of Jesus

José de Anchieta

The Holy Night

At last, oh most Holy Mother,
the great skein of time undone,
the happy hour of the birth has come,
the hour you longed for with all your heart:
holy night,
the only one brighter than day!
Oh night, lovelier than all days:
            illuminated night
with the glory of such wondrous birth!
Night in which the eyes of true light gleam
shimmering more than the sun's rays!
Night that unravels wretched darkness
restoring true colors to all the world!
God emerges swaddled in the frail body of a child,
after being locked away nine months
            in a Virgin's treasure chest.
            Oh, happy Virgin!
What joys played arpeggios on your heartstrings
            in the silence of that night!

When before your eyes on the ground appeared
the tiny infant,
come forth from the lips of the Father before the Morning Star.
He issued from your womb, dressed in your flesh,
without treading on your purity.
Such was the promise of God's messenger,
who, in your fear, greeted you
with a triumphant Hail!
With that condition you meekly surrendered
to the Divine Plan
and your trust was not misplaced.
God immediately entered your womb,
and the flower of your purity did not fade.
Now he likewise issues forth from your holy of holies,
never touching the drapes of your wedding bed.
The first mysteries are crowned with the last,
and in the silence of your heart you treasure
the sweetest joy.
Much more beautiful you have become
when he without effort or sound
passes through the cloister of your maidenhood.
Happy night, full of charm
that turned your face into a radiant star!
Aurora, while blushing with a virgin's blush,
covering the fields with new light,
shines even more lovely
when the rising sun lifts its countenance from the sea.
Just as the future Mother of the Word was born,
the morning broke, and the shadows fled.
But before the divine Sun alighted
on your virgin womb,
your brightness still lacked his wondrous light.
But when he did, your grace increased,
your light grew brighter
with shining rays of a hidden light.
Now that God,

fount of all light, born to the world
spreads the rays of his beauty,
            your luminous clarity,
oh Virgin Mother, shines all over the earth.

The Manger

How wonderful to peruse with the mind
all the phases of his birth,
to penetrate the streets of this city of God.
Admiring the manor that welcomed our Lord,
the palace where Christ the King dwelled,
the soft pillow where he laid his child's head,
his Mother's holy friends and servants,
            the songs and melodies
that lulled the Divine Child . . .
He is born in Bethlehem, sheltered in an old hut:
naked, the barren earth welcomes his birth.
The manger turned crib:
ox and donkey on either side.
Silently, a venerating old man
            takes in the gaze on his face.
            The young Mother rejoices,
the baby sweetly coos,
the heavens rejoice with unheard song.
And you, my soul, benumbed!
Why don't you visit that marvelous palace,
            that sacred refuge?
Go, no harsh warden will expel you from the threshold,
nor will he slam the door on your face.
There's no gate this to hovel, sweet resting place of beasts;
the cold freely seeps in.
You shall enter a roofless humble dwelling
            with a ceiling full of smoke,
a reed-covered hut.

The Wait

Catch a glimpse of the Mother, exuding
divine majesty,
careful in her actions, when her sweetness is born.
Allow me, o Virgin,
to recall the mysteries of that holy night,
the purest joys of your soul,
contemplating with the mind's eye all you do,
taking in avidly all you say.
The hour of the birth has come:
the icy night falls silent
and crosses the zenith's highest point.
Everywhere sleep starts to liberate
exhausted limbs:
on earth only the light of your eyes shines.
Long ago you solved the sublime mysteries,
and you seek only to gaze upon the beauty of your Child.
You ready your slight arms
that will embrace his frame,
and the bosom that will warm his chilly limbs.
You long to drink the kisses from his rosy lips,
and press your lips against that sweet face.
Gently you squeeze out the milk
from your full breast,
that the sweet lips of your tender Child will drink.
You call with humble voice
to the Father of endless glory,
with a sweeter voice still,
you call the Son:

The Prayer of Ecstasy

"Hark! The happy hour of his birth draws near,
oh glory, oh sweetness, oh God,
my heart's desire!
Now your Son will come as a light for the world,
and in the tatters of our flesh he will touch
the naked earth.
Precise was all that from heaven was brought
to me by your winged angel:
his words did not betray my trust.
I obeyed and conceived the Word in my womb
and rested assured in my virginity.
Heavenly Father, my integrity keep safe,
as I now give birth:
May it be sweet and immaculate!
You, dear Son, should I wrap in my embrace?
You, in my bosom, should I embrace you
tenderly?
You, sweet Child, will I nurse
at my breast?
Will the snow of my milk give you
sweet kisses too?
He is now born, oh God Supreme, to become my paradise!
Come with tiny tender lips to give me your heavenly kiss!"
And while you spread the flame of love divine
and wait for the birth of your pledge,
dressed in human flesh the Word is born,
and you remain a virgin.

The Happy Hour

And like from the green stem the shining flower
blooms, without injuring its lush green;
like the sun passes through glass with its threads of light
            and without harm
shoots and withdraws its rays:
The Prince of Heaven emerges from the portal of dawn,
            without opening a door,
            without tearing a seal.
From his majestic bed the spotless husband issues forth,
bringing the ring of eternal love to the new wife.
What joy now takes hold of your breast most chaste;
            what happiness, good mother,
            rocks your soul!
What new light now floods your eyes,
fixed on the birth of your God!
What do you do now with the child resting
            on the hard ground, jabbed by bitter winter cold?
You rise, your face bathed in heavenly light,
            and fall to your knees at his feet.
Thus, kneeling, your face turned to the ground,
            you worship first his divinity,
to then tumble into a sweet embrace.
You avidly drink the honey of love
            of your divine Infant
and, strumming your own heartstrings, you play this song:

Prayer of the Mother to her Newborn Son
Greatness and Smallness

"O Almighty God,
whom the great machine of the world
            proclaims as Lord and Maker,

Whose immense Glory generates in him
unparalleled light,
you who are dressed in light as in a natural cloak:
You, whom the heavens could not contain
in their vast dome,
were enclosed in the narrow coffer of my womb!
Sweet child, you left my tabernacle,
and now you lay, oh my light, on darkest ground!
Was it not your mighty hand
that tore the universe out from the void?
Is it not you whom from pole to pole the earth serves?
Why did you choose for your birth so unworthy a place?
Why were you not born in a royal chamber?
You dress the sky in stars
and the animals in their varied skins,
the fields in green grass:
And you, in turn, naked, crying and shuddering on the hard ground . . .
and from your tender eyelids the cold-blooded winter
squeezes out tears?
Oh, my Son, heaven's glory, like our Father in Heaven,
lovely you were born from my womb!
Oh, my joy, what terrible pain pierces
a mother's soul,
witnessing such torment!
How shall I lift you from the cold earth, Son?
How shall I touch with my hands your holy limbs?
Ah! I'm terrified of my unworthiness,
and your glory,
only Begotten Son of God, prevents me from touching you.
But if the cold should be thus let to batter you,
the hard earth injure your tender flesh,
more merciless my heart would be
than the harsh cold,
harder the hardness of my breast
than that of the very stone!

A Mother's Flight

I will then touch, dearest Child, your flesh,
that I alone took from my virgin flesh.
I'll satisfy my innermost love
            warming your body,
delighting in the flame that consumes my soul.
Around your cradle forever
            I'll render you service,
all that a mother's heart can imagine.
Come, then, sweet child
(and, saying this, you take him,
wrap him in swaddling clothes and nurse him).
Come, my light and my glory!
Don't refuse a mother's loving arms!
With these cloths, oh author and master of the world,
I will cover your sweet limbs.
May your hardest penury our poverty
            enrich, lavishing graces on our beggar hearts!
You give life to man,
pasture to cattle, grain to the birds,
and even the lowly worms your hand does feed.
The princes of heaven your crumbs satisfy,
and the whole universe feeds from your hand.
And now you are tormented
by merciless hunger and burning thirst:
such meager sustenance my bosom provides!
            Turn, then, oh lovely Child,
consume this overflowing breast:
feed, oh child, on your mother's milk!
A gift from your Father, issuing from my breast,
to quench the thirst that burns your lips.
Don't ask for more: this is enough:
            since you made me your mother
            and chose to be my child.
The flame of your love melts my being

and a fervent shudder pierces my bones,
as I gaze upon you, Author of life,
with your tiny lips latched on to my breast
suckling on your humble sustenance.
Cradled here in my arms I sustain you,
God-Man, glory of the highest heaven!
        I, a mother to you, my child,
        I, a daughter to you, my Father
        I, a slave to you, my Lord!
Oh lovely child, God of my whole heart!
of my life, happy life and sweet love!
Mother above all mothers, happy and chosen
among the many
to conceive this incommensurate pledge.
Your birth is the height of greatest joy:
and the greatness of my glory has no limits.
        In giving birth to you, my God,
the snow-white splendor of virginity
joined the glory of motherhood.

Mother of a Poor Little One

But as here I see you, Lord, in this humble abode,
plagued by poverty and cold,
forlorn, destitute, naked, needy,
barely finding this poor spot:
Oh sweet Son, in floods of tears . . .
(my weeping floods your lovely face).
What regal bed would welcome your majesty?
Where the warmth and comfort of a home?
Here no purple bedspread gleams,
no drapes of gold-embroidered silk,
no soft and warm woolen bed awaits,
where your poor mother might lay you down.
The birds of the air have nests,

and foxes have their dens,
to shelter them and their young.
And you, Lord of Heaven, Father of the universe,
have not a place to lay your noble head.
Oh, that you could sweetly lay
    in your mother's arms
and in my bosom mildly sleep!
But you long only for roughness and pain:
it's in kings' palaces where softness dwells.
You wanted a narrow manger as your crib
and a handful of straw as your sheets.
Rest thus here, amid the breath of beasts:
how sweet your sleep amid the hay!
And while soft sleep embraces you,
    caressing your tender eyes,
my breast will fill with your sweet snow.
My virgin womb awaits, oh lovely Child,
your thirst to quench, your hunger, satisfy.
    Sleep, Jesus,
    sweet lover and beloved,
oh countenance, paradise to my eyes!"

Glory and Peace

Thus you cradle, happy mother, your little son:
your soul cannot contain the joy that overcomes you.
Your little one, your glory, rests on the hay
    and, by His side, you
reflect his heavenly light.
A multitude of angels sing victorious,
celebrating the Nativity of their Lord.
Resounding their unending praises,
    a limpid voice stands out:
"Honor and glory and praise to God in heaven most high,

and peace on earth peace, serene and victorious
            to all the merciful hearts!"
Darkness tears open, night shines through resplendent,
and day breaks at the birth of the true Sun.
            Shepherds rush
            to adore the newborn
that the voice from heaven announced to them as their God.
As you witness this your heart overflows;
            everything increases your glory,
and all these words, you treasured them in your heart.

Song of a Young Shepherd

I too, if you allow me,
want to bow down to earth, body and soul,
before the manger of the newborn King.
I wish to present in humble song my praise
to the tender infant and to you, Virgin Mother,
            Confident, I draw near:
you, Mother will not have the heart to send me away
            nor your son see me with threatening eyes.
            But who could sing
of what came forth from the bosom of the eternal Father
before the centuries and worlds were?
            It is safer to be silent:
at times silence is God's greatest praise!
            To you, therefore, Oh Mother
this poor servant brings humble gifts,
            if your Son will allow.
And why should He not allow it, He who gave you all,
who gave himself up, the first fount of all good?
What breast could encompass your greatness,
that lips will sing the dowry of your body,
            the dowry of your soul?

So great is the heavenly light that comes forth from your heart,
that stuns the universe with your beauty.
Even the very host of heaven marvel
    that you enclosed
    the vastness of God in your chaste womb.

José's Sandals

Paulo Coelho

A long time ago, so many years ago that we can no longer remember the exact date, there lived in a village in the south of Brazil a little seven-year-old boy called José. He had lost his parents when he was very, very young and had been adopted by a miserly aunt who, even though she had lots of money, spent almost nothing on her nephew. José, having never known the meaning of love, assumed that this was simply the way life was and so it didn't bother him at all.

They lived in an extremely affluent neighborhood, but the aunt persuaded the head teacher of the local school to take on her nephew for only a tenth of the normal tuition fee, threatening to complain to the Prefect if he declined her offer. The head teacher had no option but to agree; however, he instructed the teachers to take every opportunity to humiliate José in the hope that he would misbehave and give them a pretext for expelling him. José, having never known love, assumed that this was simply the way life was and so it didn't bother him at all.

Christmas Eve arrived. The village priest was on holiday and all the pupils had to go to mass in a church some distance from the village. The girls and boys walked along, chatting about what they would find the next day beside the shoes they left out for Father Christmas: fashionable clothes, expensive toys, chocolates, skateboards, and bicycles. Since it was a special day, they were all well-dressed, all except José, who was wearing his usual ragged clothes and the same battered sandals several sizes too small (his aunt had given them to him when he was four, saying that he would only get a new pair when he was ten). Some of the children asked why he was so poor and said they would be ashamed to have a friend who wore such clothes and shoes. Since José had never known love, their questions and comments didn't bother him at all.

However, when they went into the church, and he heard the organ playing and saw the bright lights and the congregation in their Christmas finery, saw families gathered together and parents embracing their children, José felt he was the most wretched of creatures. After communion, instead of walking back home with the others, he sat down on the steps of the church and began to cry. He may never have known love, but only at that moment did he understand what it was to be alone and helpless and abandoned by everyone.

Just then, he noticed another small boy beside him, barefoot and apparently as poor as he was. He had never seen the boy before and so assumed that he must have walked a long way to get there. He thought: "His feet must be really sore. I'll give him one of my sandals. That will at least relieve half of his pain." Although José had never known love, he knew about suffering and didn't want others to experience it too.

He gave one of his sandals to the boy and returned home with the other one. He wore the sandal first on his right foot and then on his left, so that he didn't bruise the soles of his feet too badly on the stones along the way. As soon as he reached home, his aunt noticed that he was wearing only one sandal and told him that if he didn't find the other sandal the next day, he would be harshly punished.

José went to bed feeling very afraid because he knew what his aunt's punishments were like. He lay all night trembling with fear, barely able to sleep at all, and then, just as he was about to drowse off, he heard voices in the front room. His aunt rushed in, demanding to know what was going on. Still groggy from lack of sleep, José joined their visitors and, in the middle of the front room, saw the sandal he had given to the little boy. Now, however, it was surrounded by all kinds of toys, bicycles, skateboards and clothes. The neighbors were shouting and screaming, declaring that their children had been robbed, because when they woke up, they had found nothing beside their shoes at all.

At this point, the priest from the church where they had celebrated mass the previous day arrived all out of breath: on the steps of the church a statue of the Baby Jesus had appeared, clothed entirely in gold, but wearing only one sandal. Silence fell, everyone present praised God and his miracles, and the aunt wept and begged for forgiveness. And José's heart was filled with the energy and the meaning of Love.

Argentino

Terri Hinte

Marcos and Marinha Nascimento were taking me to a Christmas party. I had arrived in Belo Horizonte the night before, our visit having been arranged by Zé, my host in Rio. True to his promise, they made me warmly welcome.

Laconic Marcos, with his cap of tight black curls and wiry frame, stood in contrast to his copper-haired wife, affectionate and expansive and *gordinha* (a little meat on her bones). The couple's three children shared Marinha's ruddy coloring, especially the toddler Hipolita, a Titian cherub; the kids and their friends watched my every move, this blonde *Americana* with her inexplicable Rio accent. From the Nascimentos' modest apartment, filled with the creations of painter and craftsmen friends, I took in the rolling emerald expanse of Belo, capital of the mountainous interior state of Minas Gerais.

As we arrived at the party at the home of the Passarinhos that perfect summer evening, I felt the gears in my brain start grinding in preparation for social chatter. My Portuguese served me well enough one-on-one but tended to stall when required to produce quick banter in large groups. Marinha was my safe harbor while I sized up this gathering.

I found the refreshments and helped myself to a cold *chopinho*, then walked outside for some air. Typically, the Passarinhos' house was enclosed by a high solid wall that afforded security and privacy from the street. Partygoers were thus mingling in the front and side yards, the sultry air perfumed by jasmine, the flamboyant trees in flagrant scarlet bloom.

Strings of tiny lights illuminated the yard as darkness finally fell and the music rose from background to main event. The irresistible sounds of samba brought a number of people to their feet, and started mine itching as I sat sipping my beer. It wasn't long before I was invited to dance, by an ardent bear of a man named Tadeu. He was sweaty and sour-smelling and a bit drunk, but I was quite thrilled to be up and moving with the crowd. Tadeu, in fact, was dancing by himself, off in his own sensory world, and so, therefore, was I. But that was fine with me. In a fundamental way, I had traveled eight thousand miles to be doing exactly this, seeking some kind of intimate knowledge of the samba, with the body as hierophant and the soul the ecstatic recipient of its gifts.

While conversing with the rhythms on the dance floor in the vicinity of the frenetic Tadeu, I scanned the yard, savoring the styles of the dancing couples. One man in particular was making the samba all his own with movements of wonderful finesse and a captivating swing (or *sue-wing-ghee*, in the local parlance). As soon as the record was over, I bade Tadeu *adeus* with a thank-you-man and wasted no time in approaching the evening's prize dancer.

"*Quer dançar*?" I proposed, a bit breathless with anticipation.

"*Lógico*," he smiled, taking my hand. But of course!

His right hand alighted on my blue-draped hip, my left on his shoulder; our remaining hands found each other high in the air, laced loosely, as hips and legs and feet began to respond in unison to the tensile rhythms. It was simple, and sublime.

We introduced ourselves not long into our maiden dance—his name was Argentino, a handsome man of mocha complexion, slender build, and uncommon grace. He described himself as a poet. I was Teresa the *Americana*, as usual the only one present and therefore charged with the burden of explaining American politics. But Argentino offered instant expiation; like everyone I'd met in Brazil, he brightened at the mention of San Francisco, my home base, and offered the requisite compliments on my Portuguese ("*Você fala muito bem*!").

Frankly, though, talking got in the way of the purity of the dance. We were a team now. As each record ended, we remained poised for the next, grinning, relishing our glorious calibration.

Doubtless there are men in the world who love to dance and are good at it and who can lead a woman partner through an experience where two are one and aren't even thinking about taking off their clothes. I had just never met such a man. Dancing with men meant dancing near them or at them, as with Tadeu, or leading them, as with my American friend Jim, who could expertly follow my every step and spin.

But here with Argentino, it wasn't even a matter of his leading me; it was more like his moves *were* my moves, we were just making them together at precisely the same moment. Moreover, his *sue-wing-ghee* was of a piece with mine—closer to the pulse of the music, right in it rather than spurting out from it. Peripherally I could see many such gushing dancers in the yard, exhausting themselves after one go-round. Argentino and I, we kept percolating, marveling at the persuasiveness of a hip with intent, exploring the rich dimensions of movement in the smallest possible space. We *were* the heartbeat of samba.

How many hours passed? We hadn't left each other's company all evening, nor had the smiles left our faces. But the music had quieted down, the party was rapidly thinning out, *madrugada* was settling in. Marinha and Marcos were saying their goodbyes to the Passarinhos, and that meant I would have to bid farewell to Argentino.

We faced each other with this task, still aglow. "*Você dança como um anjo*," I said helplessly. You angel you.

Not missing a beat: "*Aprendi esta noite contigo*," he replied, the picture of serenity. I learned tonight with you.

In English the concept of speaking *with* someone is self-evident, but in Portuguese you also learn with someone, not from them, and you dream with someone, not about them, suggesting that these are not solitary activities. Clearly Argentino and I had both dreamed of a mutual surrender to the music on a tropical Christmas night. As we danced together, we learned how to make our dreams come true.

The Parish Priest

Coelho Neto

Silent and still was the star-filled, cheerless night, with none of the noise of years past when the beloved hundred-year-old parish priest was alive, rousing the pious small village with the echoing toll of the great church bell and the festive ringing of handbells.

The glorious morning of Jesus' birth was about to dawn unnoticed. The fields were deserted, the sheds empty, and the threshing floors silent. Only a peasant or two, longing for the old days, opened their door to gaze out at the white walls of the empty rectory, or stroll through the trees beneath the infinite splendor of the starry night, like the roving specter of lost joy, wistfully strumming the guitar.

Moonlight streamed soft and diaphanous through the trees, turning to silver the smooth lake water where cattle came to drink. The stark white shuttered church was like a moonlit mirage. What a difference from previous years! At that hour, the doors would have been thrown open, releasing the sanctifying aroma of incense from thuribles, and filling the village with the sound of hymns as parishioners greeted the newborn blessed Jesus, lying quietly in the manger among the cows and donkeys. So different from other years! Anyone who had heard the quivering voice of the old parish priest telling them the mystery of Bethlehem at the end of Mass in front of the crèche—how Jesus, the Almighty King of Kings was born of the Ever Virgin Mary and laid in a manger as a Savior for all people—would have felt heartsick in the face of such sadness.

In the enclosed pens, the cattle lowed deeply, anticipating the bright morning. The dawn star glowed in the crystal-clear sky.

A lone rooster crowed in a small backyard when all at once, the thunder of the great bell broke the melancholy silence of the Christmas Eve. Soon all the bells rang out, just as they had in other years, when the beloved parish priest was alive . . .

Suddenly, the doors of the small houses opened and stunned peasants appeared in the thresholds, bareheaded and lightly clothed, with lanterns held high to light up the night.

The church doors stood wide open, revealing an interior ablaze in light.

There was great astonishment among the country folk, none daring to take a single step, as the bells continued to ring festively.

A cowhand was the first to speak:

"It must be someone from the village calling us to Mass to bring back memories of the parish priest, so God's holy night doesn't pass in silence!"

The bells rang louder and louder, and already, in front of the church, a carpet of golden light was spreading outward from the candles inside.

"Should we go?" asked the cowhand.

They all went back in search of their clubs and staffs. Then gathering together, eyes focused on the brightly lit church, they made their way toward it in a tight group, slowly and hesitantly, pausing from time to time, startled by the slightest noise.

The cowhand was in the lead, pounding his staff in encouragement.

In the distance, roosters began to crow more excitedly in the backyard coolness of dawn.

Then a cry erupted through the group: the cowhand who was leading the way had fallen face down on the church steps, calling out. Not a single man dared approach to help him, and only when they saw him stand, with outstretched arms brandishing his rough staff, did they walk on.

"The parish priest! The parish priest!" shouted the cowhand, as he climbed the steps, shaken.

And the men who had come running, stopped, ecstatic, their eyes riveted on the altar of the church, stammering, "The dead parish priest! The parish priest!"

Christmas Mass was beginning.

At the altar stood a pale old man in religious garb leaning over the Holy Book, his hands clasped together in prayer. To his left, shimmering with celestial splendor, a kneeling angel with closed wings swung a thurible. To his right, another angel, in a nimbus of light, served as acolyte. Not a sound could be heard. From time to time, the celebrant turned to bless the parishioners, his pupils glowing. Little by little, the church filled up and staffs were piled high at the door. The angels flitted from side to side without touching the ground, aloft in a delicate dance.

After the service, the priest blessed all the parishioners, and as in other years, he slowly made his way down into the middle of the crowd. Flanked by the angels, he delivered an uplifting message, relating the simple Nativity story in his fatherly manner using slow and gentle words. At last, paler than the moonlight that still shone down, he walked past the assembly, extending his icy hand for a kiss; then the parishioners watched the saintly beloved priest raise his arms in thanksgiving. Finally, he turned around and stood for a time just looking at them, a silent tear running down his white cheek. He knelt down and bowed his head and everyone followed suit.

When the peasants looked up, the church bells had fallen silent, and the walls of the church were streaked with golden sunlight. The parish priest and the angels had disappeared. The peasants looked at each other as the cowhand picked up his staff, asking:

"Where did he come from? Where did he come from?"

"From the grave, surely!" said a trembling old woman.

"From heaven," said a shepherd boy, "there are no angels on earth."

"But he was crying," said the cowhand, "and there are no tears in heaven."

"Maybe he was longing for all this," said someone in the group.

Then the cowhand sighed as he blessed himself. "If there's such longing in heaven then eternal life must be very sad."

"Very sad," they all lamented.

Then the cowhand went on: "Well, he said before he died that he would always be with us, alongside us in our suffering and our joy! He said so before he died . . ."

"He will always be with us, watching over us at our tables, at our bedsides, and at our final resting places," said a backlander.

Then, stirred by the same sentiment, they raised their grateful eyes to heaven. Jesus' morning shined brilliantly.

And that is why the Church of São José do Monte has no parish priest: the rectory is heaven, and it is always the same parish priest who comes down in spirit to bless souls and countryside.

Hymn of the Three Magi

Gonçalves Dias

Among penury and misery,
In undecorated dwelling
Here is born the God-Child
Our salvation foretelling.

Peoples and kings, adore him,
The Redeemer, born from above:
He comes to live, on Earth to suffer,
To die for the sake of our love.

The heavenly court he quits,
The rich robes of the skies to shed,
He who among men is Man,
And among the angels, Godhead.

Peoples and kings, adore him,
The Redeemer, born from above:
He comes to live, on Earth to suffer,
To die for the sake of our love.

Far from the lands of the East,
Leaving their kingdoms behind,
The Magi come, their crowns to lay
At the feet of the Child Divine.

Peoples and kings, adore him,
The Redeemer, born from above:
He comes to live, on Earth to suffer,
To die for the sake of our love.

From Happy Araby they come,
Opulent off'rings to bring.
Praise to God in the highest,
Praises to Jesus on Earth ring.

Peoples and kings, adore him,
The Redeemer, born from above:
He comes to live, on Earth to suffer,
To die for the sake of our love.

The Peal of Bells at Christmas

Moacyr Scliar

Pursued by three policemen, a man runs along the streets of a small town. He is exhausted, and desperate; it is just before dawn now and his pursuers have been hard on his trail since nightfall. They don't give up the chase. The man is panting. He trips over something, falls down, picks himself up, and starts running again, in a hobbling way.

On the verge of surrendering himself, he sees a church. He runs to it. A window happens to be open and he slips through it. In the darkness, he comes upon the handrail of a staircase; he climbs up the narrow stairs, without knowing for sure what he will find at the top. Suddenly, he feels the wind on his face. He is in the belfry. There is a huge bell there, a bell that is out of all proportion to the size of the church and the tower. It is famous, this bell (but the man does not know this), for its size.

Warily, the man peers down. He sees luminous spots—the flashlights of the policemen—shifting from place to place. The policemen are confused: they have lost his trail . . .The man smiles. He is safe. Just then he feels dizzy and he staggers; on the verge of falling, he hangs on to the rope of the bell. The enormous clapper detaches itself and comes crashing down to the narrow platform where the man is standing—and from there, it rolls down through an opening in the wall of the church. And it disappears. It must have fallen into the attic.

For a few minutes the man remains motionless, panting, his eyes closed. He recovers from his fright. He was pursued, but he saved himself; he almost fell down, and again he saved himself. He opens his eyes and smiles. He is safe.

Safe, but with a problem.

He must put the clapper back inside the bell. Otherwise, when the sexton comes to ring the bell to call the faithful to Mass, he will notice that something is amiss. And then he will climb up the stairs to the tower, for sure.

Slowly and with the utmost care, the man begins to haul on the rope. The very heavy clapper keeps coming closer. The man can hear the dull sound that it produces as it trails across the boards of the attic.

Suddenly, there is resistance. The clapper is stuck, maybe caught in a rafter. The man tugs at the rope adroitly but sharply. Nothing. The clapper is stuck. Good and stuck. It won't budge. Take it easy, easy does it, the man keeps saying to himself.

He takes stock of the situation. Should he enter the attic and free the clapper? Impossible. The opening—probably a ventilation hole—is not wide enough for a burly man like the fugitive to pass through. Thrusting his arm down the opening, he can feel the rope, but not the clapper. The attic is way below. Apparently, there is nothing else the man can do except to tug at the rope, so, that's what he does, feeling increasingly more exasperated, until finally a hard tug suddenly overcomes the resistance and the man falls on his bottom on the platform. With the rope in his hand. It has detached itself from the clapper.

The man stares in disbelief at the frayed end of the rope. And then he starts to berate himself: What an idiot I am, now I've really bungled it. I was already safe and sound, and I had to bungle the whole thing.

All of a sudden, a fit of laughter: But after all, he has nothing to do with the clapper. Or with the bell, or with the tower for that matter. He is worried for nothing. He is going to scram, that's what he is going to do now. As soon as he rises to his feet, he hears the barking of dogs and he sees the beams of flashlights: the policeman have returned. And what's worse, the day is now dawning. Soon the sexton will be here, too.

Panic-stricken, the man cringes. I'm lost, he mumbles. Completely lost.

Lost? No. He won't give up so easily. They haven't found him yet, and they won't find him. Unless the sexton, unable to strike the bell, decides to climb up the stairs to the tower.

He examines the bell. It is really colossal: a good two meters in diameter, at least as much in height. The rim, turned inward, forms a sort of lip wide enough for him to rest a foot there. The man enters the bell and climbs on the lip as if it were a running-board. Balancing himself with difficulty, he gropes about, trying to find the place from which the clapper was suspended. As he expected, he finds a metal hook. Now, all he has to do is to find an object that can replace the clapper, and then attach it to the hook.

But–what object? The man looks around him. What is he looking for? A spare clapper? There isn't one. There is nothing, there in the tower. The man climbs down the bell. He empties his pockets: a jackknife, a notebook, a few coins. Nothing that could be used as a clapper. He takes off his right boot and weighs it by hand: much too light. Maybe a brick . . . ? Using the jackknife, he furiously starts digging into the wall of the church.

Half an hour later, he gives up. He has barely made a dent in the hard roughcast. And even if he succeeded in taking a brick out, he realizes, he wouldn't be able to suspend it from the hook. And even if he were able to do so, it wouldn't work, for the brick would crumble at the first clangs of the bell.

And yet, he has to find a solution. It is growing light, and now it is impossible for him to escape. One of the policemen is mounting guard at the front of the church: They suspect that the fugitive is somewhere in there. And they are waiting for the arrival of the sexton so that they can search the church. The son-of-a-bitches, mutters the man, they don't even respect God's house.

The sexton is on his way.

He slowly walks up the street where the church is located. The policeman meets him halfway. They stand talking for a while before the main entrance. The sexton gropes for the key in his pocket; the man doesn't know what to do—he opens the door—the man still doesn't not know what to do—he walks in with the policeman—and now the man knows what to do: with the rope held firmly between his teeth, he climbs inside the bell and stands on the lip inside. He is taking the place of the clapper.

The sexton doesn't start pulling on the rope right away. He is undoubtedly waiting for the policeman to finish his search of the church. Motionless inside the bell, and holding on to the hook, the man waits tensely—and what's worse, with his bladder about to burst: oh God, don't let me piss in my pants.

Finally, there is a vigorous thug at the rope; it is the sexton. Imitating the movement of the clapper, the man begins to move his head to and fro. Suddenly now!—he throws his head against the bronze.

It is an excruciating pain, an explosion inside his head—but he has produced a beautiful clang: clear, resounding, indistinguishable from the sound that the bronze clapper would produce. But the man has no time to rejoice at the outcome, or even to rest for a moment. The sexton continues to pull on the rope, and the man again strikes the bell with his head, then again, and again, and again. Twelve strokes of the bell in all.

Dizzy, his head bursting with pain, the man climbs down the bell and he stretches himself out on the small platform of the tower. He lies there, unable to move, the strokes of the bell still resonating in his skull.

Finally he opens his eyes, and he takes a peep at the street down below. The faithful are beginning to arrive to hear Mass. As for the policeman, he is gone. The man sighs. He then becomes aware of the wetness on his leg: he has just pissed in his pants.

He never leaves the place again. He has made the tower into his permanent home. He lives on pigeons, mice, and bats; he drinks rainwater.

And he strikes the bell. In the course of time, he gets used to striking the bell. His skull, although deformed from the blows, has acquired the rigidity of metal. The man doesn't envy the lost clapper, a mere article of bronze. And, one could say, he is even happy.

There is only one period of time during the year when the man really suffers: on Christmas Eve. The sexton, habitually indolent, is then suddenly seized by a burst of energy and he starts pulling on the rope like a madman. The man has to strike the bell desperately. In the midst of his agony, he even has visions: He is lying in a manger, like the Infant Jesus, and he laughs and claps his hands. Except that the three men kneeling before him are not the Three Wise Men. They are the policemen who once pursued him as far as the church.

Merry Christmas

Patrícia Melo

The university's maintenance staff follow a fixed schedule. Today, ordinarily, it would be Núbia's turn but, as it's the Christmas period, they'd decided that Neide, the eldest of the group, would do the honors.

After so many years there, Neide knows, the point is to know the lab's calendar in detail. The rabbits are put down from the twelfth week onward. After the experiments, the animals must all be placed in clean plastic bags and stored in the freezer, to be sent later on, with the rest of the hospital's disposable waste, for incineration.

On this Friday the 23rd, the operating room has been reserved for Roger, a professor in the Applied Exercise Physiology department. Neide likes him. He is systematic and quiet; he's never created problems for her. She knows all the professors in the department, as well as the names of their partners and children, information which can facilitate an animal's removal without adhering strictly to the protocol.

By now it is twenty past six and Neide has already swept and mopped the floor with disinfectant. She's hoping she'll also be able to clean the trays inside the cages before the professor comes in. For her this is the key: pleasing her employers. Which means being helpful, not only doing the tasks formally allotted to her but going above and beyond. In fact, the cleaners are neither obliged nor authorized to look after the animals. But Neide has learned from experience that replacing the sawdust in the cages and topping up their water helps secure the researchers' goodwill. She teaches the new girls joining the system that this rule holds for all the professors. They never treat the staff badly. What's more, the one who was on the point of being fired last year is running the department now. The wheel always turns. Those who were at the bottom will rise. The powerful do fall. That's politics, as they say. And they conspire in the corridors. Which is why Neide takes care to have neither friendships nor enmities. In here, she likes to say, wolves can turn into lambs and vice-versa.

The lab is almost ready when Roger comes in, dressed in overalls and surgical gloves. All that's left to do is put the hay and food out on the trays.

"I'll take care of that," the professor says, seeing Neide clearing excrement from the cages. "You're already staying up late as it is."

She smiles, and notices her hands are dirty. She goes to the basin, and asks about his children, and his Christmas plans, then sees her mistake. She's talking too much. She must be careful with this one; the man is not one for chatter.

Roger is observing his lab animals. The creatures are restless, he notes. They know they're going to die, and they've known since the first day. At least they don't feel any pain, he thinks, taking one from its cage.

He carries it over to the workbench and switches the treadmill on, adjusts the speed, then sets the rabbit on the track for some exercise. Next he opens his computer and starts taking notes, which seem endless to Neide. The way he's going, she realizes, the night will be a long one.

"Everything's ready for you in there," she tells him, after a while, hoping to move things along. "May I take one of them in?"

The professor checks his watch and says he still has a report to complete and doesn't want to hold her up. "You can go, Neide. I'll do what's left, don't worry."

"You know I like doing it, Professor," she insists. "And I've no one waiting for me at home. Not even my old mutt."

The last point is true. Her dog died only a month ago; remembering how he was crushed against the city's hot tarmac like some kind of meat paste still hurt her deeply. Lately she'd been dreaming about him. Would it be right to pray for a dead dog? She must ask the pastor about this, she decides.

Now Neide reaches the cupboard where they keep the animal feed. It's her last task of the evening. After this she'll have no reason to stay without it becoming awkward. There are some researchers who open their computers on the workbenches like this, and then all they do, for hours on end, is weigh their rats and rabbits, take blood samples and prepare slides. Neide has already invited her daughter and the grandchildren. Palmira, her widowed neighbor is coming too. This is all I need, she thinks.

Without warning, Roger seems to change his mind. Although he prefers working alone, he doesn't want to snub the cleaner, so he accepts her offer to help. He asks her to fetch a syringe and catheters. After so many years, Neide is familiar with the procedures. At the professor's side, she lays out the materials and lines up sterilized instruments. "Where's the anesthetic?" Roger asks. She goes to fetch that too.

The professor chooses a rabbit and takes it to the bench in the operating room, next door.

Neide goes too and helps him to immobilize the animal, while the professor injects sodium pentobarbital into the rabbit's ear.

In just a few minutes, the animal has lost all sensation, and its stomach is surgically sliced open.

Wouldn't it be something if my students were as assiduous as the cleaner, Roger thinks. They might catch themselves learning something.

Neide observes the euthanasia procedure obediently, but her thoughts drift far away—to her dog, dead and buried in the yard. She's been avoiding going out there; she doesn't want to feel the hurt all over again. She'll not have another pet at home, that's for sure. They only die, and then she's stuck sobbing over an old mongrel dog.

"You should practice walking like my rabbits," Roger says, as he isolates one of the rabbit's kidneys. "It would do your diabetes good."

That's a joke. She already walks so much. From the bus stop to the university is a good twenty minutes. And that's twenty minutes with her knee throbbing all the way.

"You might lose a few kilos," the professor continues. "Pass the catheter, please."

Neide does as Roger asks and watches him manipulate the probe so as to clean the organ, before carrying out his analyses.

"I don't know why I don't get thinner," she says. "I hardly eat anything these days."

Roger skillfully extracts the rabbit's kidney along with the renal capsule. He washes the cortex, then cuts it in two.

"It's time to take the rabbit off the treadmill," he says, his hands covered in blood.

Neide goes back into the main room, turns off the mill and takes the rabbit back to its cage.

"Its tongue was sticking out, poor thing," she comments on her return, seeing the professor washing his hands. "May I begin?"

Roger is used to this; he knows it's no good refusing her offer. And he's concentrating now, preparing slides and making notes.

Neide starts to clean the cages. She puts all the trays into the sink to soak and pours in a disinfectant to dissolve around them. She also sterilizes the instruments used in the operation, taking them all to the sterile oven for this final step.

It takes Roger another forty minutes to put all his research material away in the freezer. As he's about to wrap the dead rabbit in its white plastic bag, Neide takes the animal from his hands.

"Let me do the rest," she says.

As soon as the professor has gone for the night, Neide sterilizes the counter with alcohol. It's late already and, taking off her own lab coat, she thinks of the two buses she still has to catch. She mustn't forget to cover the cages and top up the water bottles.

Before leaving, she tucks the dead rabbit into her bag, combs her hair and washes her hands. It's her routine. She hates the ammonia smell of the lab.

"Have you seen my phone?" Roger asks, bursting in suddenly.

Neide starts walking around the room at the professor's side, checking over the workbenches and everywhere else a cellphone could have been left behind.

Suddenly she realizes that she's leaving a trail of blood behind her. The liquid is seeping out of her canvas bag, and oozing through her blouse and trousers too. She clasps her bag abruptly to her, panicked and embarrassed, as if this might somehow staunch the flow.

The professor appears unsurprised. For an instant, the pair stands facing each other in silence, their eyes fixed on the ground.

Roger gives a long sigh. He says "Neide," but doesn't know what should come next.

"We like to eat rabbit back at home," she confesses.

"They're packed full of chemicals, full of poison," Roger says.

"We enjoy it," Neide says, still afraid to meet his gaze.

"Has it been a while?"

She nods.

"It won't do your health any good," he says again.

"It doesn't bother me, Professor. We like it."

Another silence.

"You shouldn't be doing this," he repeats.

And walks away to the exit. He's already at the door when Neide asks if he's going to report her.

"No," he answers.

"You're a good man," she says. "Merry Christmas."

"Merry Christmas," he replies.

And lets the lab door bang closed.

Christmas

Virgílio Várzea

It was Christmas Eve in Joinville, the charming German-Brazilian city at the northeastern tip of the state of Santa Catarina. Twilight's last rosy glimmers were gradually fading to the west over the plains bordering the Cachoeira River where, in picturesque clusters of foliage, the vast green mangrove swamps gave rise to sprawling tree fronds and slender, twisted trunks of eucalyptus, opening their wind-whipped bunches of leaves to the pale afternoon sky.

The *D. Francisca*, the tiny steamer I was on, had already rounded one of the wide loops of the river when, through gaps in the greenery, I began to catch a glimpse of the red slate roofs on the white-walled houses of the City of Princes. Just a few moments later, the dense mangrove hedges that surrounded the swift vessel sailing upstream suddenly disappeared, and Joinville's main quay came into focus—a gray line of stonework, topped by a row of warehouses.

I quickly navigated one of the stone stairways, my valise in hand, amid a noisy and festive crowd of locals, men and women shouting and laughing in a Portuguese full of *r*'s and harsh, guttural German syllables. They were family members and others who had come to welcome friends and acquaintances from São Francisco and Desterro on their Christmas visit to the tiny new colony across the Atlantic, which is perhaps the most beautiful city in Brazil.

A jumble of conveyances took up the entire square behind the warehouses—passenger carriages and delivery wagons, some stopped to receive parcels, others on the move, crammed with people coming and going, pulled by powerful teams of horses, to the lively crack of whips. Caught up in the scramble, I was looking for a buggy or someone to take me to Rua dos Lírios, home to a beloved German-Brazilian family, when I suddenly found myself snatched up by two sturdy arms, embracing me with warmth and affection:

"Oh mein frrriend! Oh, mein frrriend!"

It was Paulo Rosemberg, a smooth-faced, blue-eyed and very blond eighteen-year-old Hercules, my devoted comrade and youngest son of the family awaiting me on the beautiful Rua dos Lírios. With one hand grabbing my valise and the other my shoulder, the young man quickly led me to his carriage in the midst of the commotion made worse by the darkness that was fast descending.

Mounted in the stirrups, and us comfortably ensconced in the maroon cushions, the coachman prodded the horses, and we rolled down Rua do Porto, where the first few houses were already brightly lit, their gardens and whitewashed macadam festooned with large golden ribbons. Through the wide-open windows and doors of these sacred recesses of serenity and love, we could see beautiful traditional Christmas trees in the center halls, standing out like bouquets of greenery, aglow with smoky flames from tiny colored wax candles on every branch, amid a multitude of ornaments and sweets. Bunches of brightly dressed golden-haired children frolicked joyfully around each tree. Among the flowering vines that lined the verandas—and whose tiny leaves created an intricate bronze latticework against a background of soft lights—men, women, and young adults dressed in traditional German holiday attire, their heads a honeyed shade of ripe wheat or hay, gathered around long, linen-clad tables covered with large coffee cakes and an assortment of glasses and bottles; talking, laughing, and drinking fresh frothy beer or fine Rhine wines . . .

To get to the house, we had to pass through the heart of the city: Rua do Meio, Rua do Príncipe, Rua de Ludovico, Rua da Cachoeira and Rua do Norte, all of them wide, spotless expanses, with houses bordered by trimmed grass and rose hedges.

Our carriage sped along, passing dozens of others through the lively streets. Amid the rush of ornate buildings awash with light, bursting with laughter and song, glowing Venetian lanterns, and the children's beloved tree standing in the center, we could forget for a moment how solidly built they were, and just take in the dazzling sight of these amazing castles' luminous and lacy architecture, the kind the sagas tell us would glow at night throughout the fiefdoms during great royal feasts. Our impressive vehicle only slowed or occasionally stopped to make way for numerous groups of adolescent boys and girls wandering in all directions, singing along in a great choir, in which deep male voices sometimes drowned out the delicate female harmonies.

In several places, massive buildings with wide porticoes and interior courtyards, like enormous auditoriums, stood out, fantastical in the sparkle of their towering façades dotted with festive lanterns. These were the "public balls," where the people—laborers and servants—gathered to celebrate Christmas. There, bands of a hundred or more musicians performed a dizzying but impeccably tuned repertoire of polkas, country dances, and waltzes, as countless couples happily swirled in those raucous galas that begin when the first stars come out and end only at dawn.

For maybe half an hour we traveled like this, enjoying the widespread excitement of the city, where few souls, I'm sure, would miss the joy of Christmas, that distinctive and timeless celebration of the northern nations. And it was precisely as the moon rose majestically over the eastern hills where the river meanders through silver waterfalls that we joyfully turned onto the beautiful Rua dos Lírios, twinkling with light from the houses' façades.

Moments later we were warmly welcomed in front of the spacious veranda tucked between the foliage of the Rosemberg mansion. The owner, kindly old Wilhelm, along with his wife and daughters—an indescribably beautiful group of blonde Valkyries—having left the crowd of guests inside, immediately came to embrace me, ordering Paulo to take me upstairs to the assigned rooms. So upstairs we went, and after taking just enough time to shake off the coal dust from the nearly six-hour journey from São Francisco, I made my way back down, overjoyed to be introduced to family friends and pay my first visit to the Christmas tree in the great hall, where the children were making a delightful racket.

On the sweeping railed veranda opening out to the front garden, under the thick lattice of golden-lit climbing vines, stood the immense table set for the *Weinhnachten* feast, filled with men and women. At its head sat Wilhelm Rosemberg and his wife, relaxed and happy, in that sincere warmth of affection so charming in the Saxon race, delighting everyone with their lively conversation and enthusiasm. Each of the guests served themselves from the comfort of their seats, for there is not a single German home that does not give its servants time off—and Christmas is the sacred time off that no one dare violate. The men and boys were holding liter-sized porcelain or crystal mugs with shiny white metal lids tilted back over the handle: beer bubbled inside, crowned with a translucent, topaz-colored foam. The ladies and *fräuleins* nibbled on savory delicacies and sweets, accompanying tasty morsels with small sips of Kocheim and Jahannisberg, famous fine Rhine wines.

As soon as I walked up with Paulo, old Wilhelm, seated where he was, without moving, yet smiling and affable, with his lively sable eyes full of warmth and his long, gray beard, introduced me unceremoniously by shouting my name to everyone. Then he beckoned me to his side, where after paying my respects, I sat down in the chair that had just been vacated by one of his daughters, the charming Bertha, who was heading for the other room with two plates full of cake and a chilled bottle.

Clasping me by the shoulder before patting me on the back, after politely asking about my journey and my family, whom he had met when visiting Desterro, the good German said:

"Bertha taked sometink to zuh old folks, zere in zuh rrrroom vit zuh girls."

The "old folks" were the ninety-year-old Rosembergs, husband and wife, the proud parents of Wilhelm, who himself was already sixty-five. Like every year, the elderly couple, although tired and increasingly unsteady, refused to leave their "throne" in the great hall, where the grandchildren and great-grandchildren were sitting with their "tree," until the stroke of midnight. That's when the wondrous Saint Sylvester, *der Sylvesterabend*, was due to arrive with his heavy leather bag filled with Christmas gifts for the children.

We chatted, while across the table, Paulo poured me beer and helped himself to slices of cheese and coffee cake. Around the table, more than forty guests, men and women alike, were drinking and laughing in a cheerful and dignified manner. From time to time, the children's loud shouts, like a hail of firecrackers suddenly bursting into the air, could be heard from the great hall situated in the center of the mansion, separated by a room whose doorways were covered with beautiful curtains.

After a few hours, I wanted to go see the Christmas tree with Paulo, to determine its size, how it had been set up that year, and what surprises it held. But the fatherly Wilhelm put his hand on my shoulder and suggested I wait to see it when Saint Sylvester came in, which would be soon, as it was already half past eleven.

So we continued drinking beer and chatting pleasantly, when suddenly, there was a jingling of a bell outside in the back of the mansion, by the orchard. The children broke into a frenzied scramble, as if a large flock of crows had been let loose unexpectedly. All the rooms broke into an uproar, and everyone at the table, starting with Wilhelm and his wife, stood up and shouted loudly:

"Der Sylvesterabend! Der Sylvesterabend!"

Then they all rushed into the hall where the tree stood. Swept away by Wilhelm, I went along excitedly, pulsing with curiosity.

The great hall was bathed in light from the massive chandelier and golden sconces flanking each doorway, still occupied by only the elderly couple and the children. Quiet now and seated on a row of beautifully carved oak chairs, the children's blue eyes were riveted on the scarlet damask curtain hanging over the threshold of the corridor that led to the orchard veranda.

Waiting for the "saint" to appear, following one last jingle of the bell, we all formed into two groups on either side of the room. The groups then walked toward the children, starting from the small platform covered in red velvet, where the Rosemberg grandparents were sitting on two imperial high-backed armchairs with gold marquetry, in the style of Frederick the Great. They were dressed in clothes befitting another era and reflecting obsolete customs. Both were strong-boned yet thin, with broad, intelligent foreheads and the high, well-trimmed chests of the blond Baltic peoples. They had wide expressive faces wrinkled like pink parchment by the emotions of an almost century-long existence, their tiny green eyes softly twinkling, already empty of hopes and dreams, of course, but still moist with vague tenderness and a sense of longing. Their snow-white hair gave them a certain dignified air.

In the center, between the "throne" and the children, stood the tree, cut from the top of a young pine, one of those that when fully grown, cover the plateaus of São Bento and Serra do Mar in colossal forests. It was the largest of all the Christmas trees old Wilhelm had ever given his beloved children: measuring about four meters high, from its base to the hand-crafted beams of the coffered ceiling. Completely covered in lights, like a patch of starry sky, it held a variety of ornaments from the famous factories in Hamburg and Meissen, and an array of small, dried doughs and sweets representing zoo creatures and other remarkable things. The amazing splendor of the much-loved *baum* of northern European childhood captivated and delighted.

Meanwhile, in my group with Paulo, tired from the long wait and my eyes dazzled by that marvelous tree, I was lost in thought, admiring the divine innocent face of Bertha, who from the group across the room was openly gazing at me with her magical celestial eyes of crystalline blue. As I dreamed, cherishing enchanting illusions of devotion to a German woman—in a home full of purity and affection, order and harmony—I was suddenly startled awake by the jingling of a bell.

A heavy silence fell, and everyone stared anxiously at the scarlet damask-covered door. Suddenly, the curtain was drawn and gathered into folds at the side. The children stood up in a rush, and a resounding, joyful cheer rang out from every mouth:

"Der Sylvesterabend! Der Sylvesterabend!"

A towering old man then appeared in the doorway, wearing a thick gray fur coat and a large mink cap, and carrying a tall staff. His hair and beard covered his shoulders and chest in wide snowy folds, framing his noble face, where his eyes shone like two glistening turquoises. The edge of his fur coat gave way to massive legs wearing thick yellow boots, wrinkled and damp as if from splashing through snow on some Prussian plain, from where he had miraculously appeared. He was carrying a large leather bag, so big that its mouth was hidden under one armpit, while its bottom, as full and damp as a wineskin, nearly touched the floor.

With a military swagger and without uttering a word, the saintly protector of children—and burier of "old years" that plummet into the abyss with each rotation of the globe—marched, toward the "throne," circumspect and stern, without so much as a smile. There, the elderly Rosembergs stood waiting for him with their aged tremors, silent yet smiling, and shook his large hand. Then the "heavenly messenger" stopped in front of the tree, where he was immediately swarmed by the children, who, after kissing his staff, began to shout loudly, clamoring for their "goodies."

Saint Sylvester then gave a faint smile, pulling at his long beard. And bending his giant stature ever so slightly, he gently and lovingly opened his leather bag, passing out a wonderful assortment of charming toys and shiny boxes of candy to the children.

The crowd broke into applause and enthusiastic cheering for the "saint."

And in that joyful din, Saint Sylvester slowly backed away to the far end of the hall until reaching the threshold of the corridor. There, again to the sound of a jingling bell, the scarlet damask curtain hid him for another year, in that familiar childhood "mystery" that makes German Christmas such a great attraction.

Then in the vast adjoining room, the dancing began with a succession of country dances and waltzes until the first light of dawn.

Christmas Sonnet

Joaquim Maria Machado de Assis

One man—upon that friendly night,
The Christian eve of the Nazarene—
Recalled his childhood's vivid scene:
The dance, the song, each pure delight.

He yearned to capture, fresh and clean,
Those feelings in their former flight,
Upon that same old friendly night,
The Christian eve of the Nazarene.

He chose the sonnet's measured page . . . But
inspiration would not wage,
His faltering quill stood still and dry.

And fighting with each metric round,
Just one small verse at last he found:
"Did Christmas fade, or did I?"
who comes down in spirit to bless souls and countryside.

Christmas Chronicle

Luis Fernando Verissimo

—Sir, there's a gentleman here at the gatehouse who says he's Santa.
—Who?
—Santa.
—Ask who he is.
—Santa. He says he's Santa.
—Ask his surname.
—Claus.
—Tell him to stop playing around and give us his real name.
—Claus. He's saying it's Claus.
—What does he look like?
—Fat. White beard. Red clothes and hat. Boots. He's carrying a sack.
—Ask if he has ID. Ask him for his ID card.
—He says he doesn't have any, sir.
—Nothing?
—He says he has nothing.
—Ask if . . .
—He says he has a letter from Marcelo.
—Ay ay ay. How does he know my son?
—He says he doesn't. He just got his letter.
—Ask to see the letter.
—I have it here, sir.

—What does it look like? Describe it to me.

—Ok . . . A child's handwriting . . . It's a wish list. Signed "Marcelo."

—Does it have our address?

—No. Only "Marcelo."

—Ask to see the envelope.

—Yes, sir . . . Here it is. Let me see. Addressed to . . . "Santa Claus, the North Pole."

—There's no return address?

—What address?

—The sender's address.

—No. Just "Marcelo."

—Did you already let him through the gate?

—No. He's here at the gatehouse window.

—Let me talk to him.

—Yes, sir. Just a moment.

—Yes?

—Who's this?

—Santa Claus.

—What's your name, please?

—Santa Claus.

—Look, I don't have time for . . . Is this Danúsio? Is it you? Quit messing around.

—It's Santa. I'm bringing the presents your son asked for.

—Is this some kind of special promotion?

—What?

—Is this a promotion for some store? Some product? If it is, no one here is interested.

—It's Santa Claus.

—That's enough. Either you tell me who you are or . . .

—I'm Santa Claus.

—Enough! I don't know how you got our son's name and address, but you should know that we're very well protected. Did you get a good look? Very well protected. As a matter of fact, you're being filmed right now.

—I just wanted to deliver the presents, but you don't have a chimney.

—Sure. The presents you brought from the North Pole for Marcelo.

—Yes.

—Made by midgets in your workshop.

—Elves.

—Elves. Of course. At the North Pole.

—That's right.

—You speak Portuguese very well for someone who lives at the North Pole.

—Thank you.

—How do you enter the country without papers?

—I've never had a problem.

—You should know I've already sounded the alarm, understand? I pulled the alarm, and the police are on their way. If I were you, I'd take my sleigh and get out of here. Quick.

—You mean I can't come in?

—No. Do you think someone here is a child?

—Marcelo isn't a child? From the letter . . .

—Beat it while there's still time. And look, if you come near my son again, you'll be sorry. Do you hear me? We're very well protected!

—And the presents?

—What?

—What should I do with the presents?

—Get lost!

—Fine.

—The police will be here any minute. If you were smart, you'd beat it while there's still time and not show your face around here again.

—I'll leave the presents with the gatekeeper.

—You won't be leaving anything! Pass the phone to the gatekeeper.

—Okay.

—Hello?

—Mr. Valdomiro? Don't accept anything from him. The sack could have explosives. They're acting as a group. He blows up the gatehouse, and the gang comes in behind him.

—Do you think, sir?

—You can't ever drop your guard. Don't argue with me, send this bum away.

—But sir . . .

—Get rid of him!

Excerpt from

Away from Home

Rona Jaffe

Rio. At this hour the beach was not usually so deserted. But now only a few lingering bathers remained, and a group of boys playing their daily soccer game at Posto Six. The sky was streaked with the pink and blue beginnings of sunset. If you looked straight out to sea you could see only the incredible blueness of the water for miles and miles and then the striated sky. A little to the right you could see an island with a lighthouse on top of it, just beginning to blink its man-made star into the evening. Farther to the right was the five-mile curving crescent of pale sand—the beach of Copacabana. On the far left, mountains, green, brown, gray, starting to fade into blue and purple in the setting sun. It was Christmas Eve.

On the small traffic island in front of the Copacabana Palace Hotel they had just lit up the Christmas tree for the first time, and it looked a little strange and out of place: northern fir and luminescent globes in a hot tropical night. In front of the tree was the mosaic sidewalk, swirls of gray and white tiles in the manner of old Portugal. It was getting darker.

On the beach that edged the sidewalk in front of the hotel the man who sold kites had laid them to rest. They were bird-shaped kites made of cloth, great eagles, red and blue and black and white, that flew above the beach during the day in the blue sky like real birds, and in the evening perched in the sand supported by thin wooden poles. All day another man had been working too, dressed in shabby khakis, crouched in front of a giant sand castle he had built and finishing the last exquisite details of the windows with a tiny pointed stick. Now it was complete, just as the sky turned black and filled with stars. Carefully he set candles all around the sand castle and lit them, so that from across the street it looked like a mysterious shrine, all glowing. He put a painfully lettered sign in the sand in front of it: *Exact Replica of the Taj Mahal.* He had never seen the Taj Mahal except on picture postcards. There was a string of lights now all along the curve of beach, the lights that some people call The Queen's Necklace. They were streetlights, lights of hotels, of sidewalk cafés, of apartment buildings, of Copacabana and Ipanema and Leblon.

In one of the great modern apartment buildings overlooking Copacabana Beach an American couple named Helen and Bert Sinclair were sitting in their library waiting for a long-distance telephone call he had put in to the States an hour before. They were a good-looking couple, he very dark, she fair, both young, with the look of settled Americans in a foreign country: healthy, sleek, privileged, proud, and vulnerable.

Helen had lit only one lamp as the room had slowly darkened. Under the lamp on the desk the telephone rang; the long-drawn-out ring of Long Distance. "That's it," Bert said. "You take it first."

"Hello?" Helen said into the receiver, not quite sure whether or not she should shout. This was the first time they had spoken to New York.

"Helen?" her mother said. "How are you? Are you all right?"

"I'm fine. We're all fine. Can you hear me?"

"Yes, I can hear. Are you sure you're all right?"

"I'm *fine*, Mother. We called to say Merry Christmas."

"Merry Christmas, darling. Merry Christmas." She could hear her mother begin to weep. "How are Roger and Julie? I read in the papers that there's a smallpox epidemic in Brazil."

"That's the first I ever heard of it," Helen said. "The children are fine. Please stop crying, Mother, I can't hear you."

"Does Julie still have allergies?"

"No, they've gone. I wrote you that. *Please* stop crying, Mother. I can't hear *anything*." It gave Helen a sick feeling to hear her mother cry on the telephone;

it was like going down too rapidly in an elevator. And in a way, she felt angry at her mother, too, for crying now when all she and Bert had wanted was to call and make tonight a happier Christmas Eve. "How's Daddy?"

"He's fine. He's here, grabbing the receiver out of my hand. Take care of yourself, Helen. Take care of yourself, darling. Don't let the children drink that milk. They never pasteurize it. I'll send you some more powdered milk by air mail."

"Mother, that costs a *fortune*. Please don't. They *do* pasteurize some of the milk. Don't send me any more milk. Please stop crying."

"Hello, Helen!" her father said happily. "Merry Christmas!"

He sounded so hearty and cheerful and genuinely glad to speak to her that it almost made Helen start to cry herself.

"Daddy, how are you?"

"Fine. We're all fine."

"Is it cold in New York? Is it snowing?"

"It's nice and invigorating. Eight above zero. You would like it."

He wants me to come home, too, Helen thought. He knows how much I hate cold weather. "It sounds lovely," she said.

"I went ice skating this morning in the park. Your old man can still do a figure eight. I wish I could take Roger ice skating."

"And *we* wish you could come here and lie on the beach with us," Helen said cheerfully. But she was beginning to feel depressed and homesick, and she was wondering if it would have been better after all if they had not called. They could have sent a cable and avoided the pang of sensing all the unsaid things that came through those familiar voices.

"Do you still like Rio?"

"Yes."

"How's Bert?"

"He's fine. I'll let you speak to him." She held the receiver out to Bert, mouthing "Hurry."

"Hello," Bert said. "Merry Christmas. Fine. We're all fine. Thank you, same to you, sir. Hello, Mother. Merry Christmas. We're all wonderful. Thank you. Yes . . . just a minute." He cupped his hand over the mouthpiece. "Your mother wants to say goodbye."

"Oh, Mother," Helen said. "Goodbye. Have a wonderful, wonderful New

Year. Kiss Daddy for me." What she wanted, really, at that moment, was to ask to speak to her father again; but she thought of how long they had spoken on this transatlantic call already and of the money it would cost, and how none of them had actually said anything that mattered, and her throat closed with the beginning of tears. It occurred to her suddenly that her father might die, that she might never see him again or hear his voice. Her father was always so reassuring and comfortable about everything, even when she knew that he was as worried as her mother about some imaginary South American epidemic. He could say, "I miss you," and they were two people missing each other and it was honest and natural. Of course they missed each other. But then her mother would say, "I miss you," and sob, and suddenly Helen would find herself obliged to feel so sorry for her mother's bereavement that she did not miss her mother at all.

"Is Daddy all right, Mother? Are you sure?"

"He's all right. But he misses you and the children. Do you really have to stay there for three years?"

"Bert *has* to stay. We're going to say goodbye now. The children send love. Give Daddy a kiss for me. Goodbye, darling."

When she replaced the receiver her hand was shaking. *I wish we hadn't called.*

Bert smiled at her, looking a little satanic in the dark at this moment. "My God," he said. "It's a good thing we decided not to put the children on. We wait here an hour and a half for the call to come through and its costs four contos, and then everybody cries so much you can't hear anything anyway. You look like you could use a very small Scotch and water."

It was exactly what she had been thinking, but for some reason, perhaps because she felt guilty at hearing her thoughts expressed aloud, she felt annoyed at him. "You don't have to make fun of them," she said, more vehemently than she had intended.

"I'm not. I think your father's wonderful."

"And you can't stand my mother. You never could."

"I just think you ought to tell her a few things," Bert said coolly. "You're a big girl now. You have two big children."

"And I'll *always* worry about my children, even when they're grown up. That's the way mothers are built. If you're a mother, you're a mother in your head too. Otherwise you shouldn't be one."

"Alright," he said. "Excuse me. Do you want a Scotch?"

"No, thank you."

"Well, I do." He walked to the door, not looking back.

"Please!"

He turned then, and when she looked at his face that was so beautiful to her, and remembered that this man would belong to her forever, no matter what ridiculous things they might say to each other in anger, she almost hated herself. "I do want a Scotch," Helen said, very softly. "Wait and I'll come with you."

They walked to the living room hand in hand, and Bert made two very stiff Scotches at the bar. "What's that silly thing they always say here?" she asked.

"*Chin-chin.*"

"Yes. It sounds Chinese, not Brazilian." They touched their glasses together. The first taste of Scotch and water was good and Helen drank it all quickly, feeling herself beginning to unwind. It had been stupid to get upset. Relatives always wept at things like long-distance calls on holidays, and weddings, and christenings, because of the whole fabric of emotion that has been woven about these events, not because anyone is genuinely moved. It was a mild form of hysteria. It was stupid to get upset about it. They had been alone here for almost a year and they would remain here over two years more, and there was nothing to be done about it. No one had put a gun at hers or Bert's head and said, "You *must* go to Brazil." They had come here by choice, for the money, for the adventure, for the chances Bert would have when he eventually returned to the States. They had wanted to come. And when they finished the three years here they would probably go to another country, like Colombia, for another three years, and only then would they go home.

She put her arms around her husband's waist. "Do you love me?"

"Yes."

"*Muito?*"

"Yes."

"*Demais?*"

He smiled. "Yes."

"Do you think I'm an old, boring mother of two—what you said—two big children ?"

He put his hands on the small of her back and then slid them lower, pulling her to him. "No, I think you're the young, beautiful mother of two little, tiny, midget children."

"Hold me there. I like that."

"Hold me too. Just for a minute."

Just for a minute, Helen thought; like two guilty teenagers necking in the parlor. She looked into his eyes and knew that he was thinking the same thing. It's very nice to tell children about sex but you mustn't act it out for them. The children will finish their dinners and run in any minute. When you have children you *are* a Mother, you *are*, with a capital M; and you have to make love at night when they're sleeping, or when they're away, and things are never just the same.

"I'm thinking of something I'm going to do to you tonight," Bert said.

"We have to go to that damned party," she whispered against his mouth.

"After the party."

I hate it, Helen thought; I hate it, I hate it. Eat on schedule, sleep on schedule, play with the children on schedule, even make love on schedule. Not when you *want* to, but when everything else is neatly disposed of and it's time. Is that all life has turned into for us?

"What's the matter?" Bert asked when she drew away slightly.

"Nothing, darling," she said gently. She kissed him and drew away farther, pretending to look for a cigarette. "I thought it was supposed to be the *men* who don't like to begin things they can't finish. I think it's the women too."

He lit cigarettes for them both and gave her one. "Do you think we ought to eat something before this dinner tonight?"

"Not unless you're hungry now. They're Americans, so they'll serve early. I figured out a whole timetable. There are the Americans who say, 'We always eat at six-thirty, just like at home,' with that tiny bit of comfortable smugness in their voices; and then of course they have to serve a whole buffet at midnight anyway. And then there are the Embassy people and the others who've semi-adapted, and they have dinner at eight or eight-thirty. And then there are the Brazilians, who have dinner at ten."

"Or twelve or one," Bert said wryly.

"All right, love, I can take a hint. I'll have Maria make you a sandwich. Margie and Neil are coming over for a drink first, and then we'll drive to the party in their car, if you want. It's sport shirts tonight."

"Good."

She went into the kitchen to talk to the maids, and then into Julie's room where the children were finishing their supper with the governess. It occurred to her fleetingly as she walked down the hall, pressing a light switch, picking up a book that Roger had left on the hall chair, that she had turned into a kind of major-domo. Menus, lists, social schedules, clothes, orders to servants—she sometimes felt as if she were running a small hotel. During the years in their apartment in Riverdale, and then in the house in Westport when the children were older, she had done her own work with only a twice-weekly cleaning woman to do the heavy jobs. Looking back, she realized she had probably done the work of five, but all her friends had done the same so none of them had really thought it was extraordinary. And now she was only the giver of orders to others, and she felt ten years older.

Margie and Neil Davidow came at seven, wearing that polished, brushed look of people who have just dressed for a party. She was a smallish, dark girl, with an excellent figure and an even more spectacular clothes sense, and an incredible neatness and femininity of person that passed for beauty and actually managed to substitute very well for it. Many people said she was beautiful. Very quietly, Margie was a typical product of the twentieth century. She had had her teeth straightened while she was in high school, and her nose shortened a year later, and she wore invisible contact lenses for her nearsightedness. She had no children, and her husband had money, so she spent most of her time taking care of herself and her husband; choosing soft material to have his suits made, finding an obscure Italian tailor to cut them better than anybody else. She was twenty-five and Neil was thirty-one, the same age as Bert Sinclair. But Neil Davidow looked much older than Bert, not because of his features but because he had a kind of settled look. He was tall, with large features and dark straight hair. Until Margie had told her, Helen had never been able to guess how old Neil actually was. Neil and Margie had been married for five years, three of them spent in Brazil, and Margie Davidow was Helen Sinclair's best friend.

As soon as greetings had been exchanged the two couples separated; the men to the bar to make fresh drinks, the women to the corner of the sofa.

"Look at us," Helen said, laughing. "The men on one side of the room and the women on the other. God forbid someone should flirt with someone else's wife."

"I'll tell Neil to come over and flirt with you," Margie said cozily. "He'll love it." She waved at her husband. "Come here, darling, we need you."

"What are you talking about anyway?" Helen said. "Money or women?"

"Money," said Neil.

"Women," said Bert. "Be quiet, you'll have them too sure of us."

"Well, at least give Bert some good tips on the market, Neil," Helen said.

"That's what I'm doing," said Neil.

How he lights up when he talks about business, Helen thought. And look at my husband. They look as if they're off on a treasure hunt. "Don't you want a drink, Margie?"

"No. No, thank you. We'll have to drink at the party, and it's too hot tonight."

"Listen," Helen said, "Roger is going to flip tomorrow when he sees that train you and Neil gave him. You shouldn't have spent so much money. I never saw a train like that in Brazil."

"I sent to F.A.O. Schwarz for it," Margie said. "Why not, anyway? By the time you all go back to live in the States he'll be too old for trains. And I adore him."

"Oh, how he adores you, too!"

"I really ought to have children," Margie said vaguely. She turned her gold bracelet around on her wrist and looked at it as if she had never seen it before. "I can, you know. There's nothing wrong with me. I just . . . never decided to." She lowered her voice. "I had two martinis in the kitchen before we came here. You might have gathered."

"You look fine," Helen said.

"Neil got a letter from his mother today and she made another one of those awful coy remarks about how nice it would be to be a grandmother. I hate it."

"I hate it too. Luckily for me I had Julie right away, so all I had to put up with was 'Oh, you're too young, too young, what a *shame*!'" She and Margie grinned at each other companionably. Then Margie's smile faded.

"There are limits to everything," she whispered vehemently. "I don't care what anyone tells me. You can tell me my shoes clash with my dress, or my new tablecloth is ugly, or I ought to learn more about politics. All right. Okay. I'm not a brilliant person, I'm just an ordinary person, and I'll thank anyone who wants to tell me something if it's going to help me improve. But there's one thing I can't stand. Nobody is going to tell me when I'm going to do my screwing with my husband, *nobody!*"

Helen looked at Margie, troubled. She had never seen her so excited. She covered Margie's hand, where it lay on the couch, with her own. "Of course not."

"I'm just drunk," Margie said lightly. She smiled, and she looked the same as before her outburst—unruffled, serene, ladylike, not even a bit of face powder beginning to wear off. "You know," she said quietly, "sometimes, like this evening before we got here, I wish I were dead."

Neil Davidow was looking at his watch. He came over to the sofa and smiled at Margie, reaching out to pull her to her feet. "Come on," he said. "We have to go. We'll be late."

"We'll all take our car," Margie said. "All right?"

Helen looked at both of them, Margie encircled lightly by her husband's arm, looking up at him with an expression that could only be honest affection, warmth and pleasure, Neil with his before-party look that showed he knew he was going to have a good time no matter what happened. In many ways, except for being childless, they were the most conventional couple Helen knew. And yet there was sorrow there, and suffering, and something worse, she suddenly realized, some kind of secret that one held away from the other. "Come and say goodnight to your brats," Helen said, taking Bert by the hand. "I promised them."

Margie and Neil came too, and as she watched Margie kissing Roger and Julie, Helen wondered briefly if she herself were the kind of unpleasant mother who showed off the delights of motherhood to her less fortunate friends. She hoped it wouldn't look that way to Margie. She felt a kind of wariness for a moment in the presence of her friend who was dear to her and could be hurt by something completely unwitting and innocent. But Margie seemed perfectly happy, and when they all went down in the elevator she was already fussing with the back of her hair to be sure the humidity had not spoiled her set and you would not think she had another thought in her head. God, Helen thought, I'm glad I have a happy marriage. I'm glad I can know that it's always going to be there, that it's always going to be the same.

The party they went to was given by an American couple named Mildred and Phil Burns, who were both in their mid-thirties and came from Chicago. They were known to their friends as Mil and Phil. Mil was the sort of woman, as Margie Davidow had once put it, who always walked into a room where there were strangers and said, "I'm Mil Burns and this is my husband." When she was eighteen years old she had been Corn Queen at Iowa State College, and she had been allowed to sit on a float surrounded by her handmaidens in white dresses. Her husband sometimes mentioned this when talking about old times back in the States, but Mil never talked about it. She had gained twenty pounds and a husband and three children, and the past was rather silly, but when she walked she held her head up stiffly, partly to show her handsome profile, partly to minimize her double chin, and partly so that her invisible crown would not slide off.

Phil Burns had arrived in Rio six months before his wife, and had rented their apartment, arranged for the necessities, set up his business, and then sent for his family. Mil had arrived protestingly, hating the apartment, hating the climate, hating the cockroaches, hating the telephone system, hating the tan bath water. They had been in Brazil now for more than a year, and Phil loved it as much as Mil did not. He was one of those enthusiastically overassimilated Americans who say things like "I know a wonderful little bar where you can go if you don't want to meet anyone you know—because only American tourists go there." He always carried a copy of the South American edition of *Time* magazine, and he said, "No?" at the end of questions that he asked in English.

Mildred met them at the door. The living room was already filled with people, talking and smoking, and a white-coated butler walked about with a tray of highballs. "You don't mind if you have to introduce yourselves?" Mil said. "I'm hoarse. I've been yelling at the maids all day. They're so stupid. I tried to tell them how to make a decent looking hors d'oeuvre, but they can't learn."

"I think they look beautiful," Helen said, taking an infinitesimal pie filled with hot-flavored shrimps from a tray on the coffee table.

"You're crazy, Mil," Margie said. "You always worry too much."

"Heleninha!" Phil Burns said, putting an arm around Helen's waist. He pronounced it *Eleneenya*. He was a little shorter than his wife, and he had a boyish, Ivy League look, a crewcut graying at the temples, and earnest, sad eyes. Helen liked him. "There are some people here you don't know," Phil said. "There's a Brazilian—see—over by the window talking to the woman in the flowered dress. His name is Nestor and he's extremely interesting, you ought to talk to him. And there's Trainer Wilkes, from the Embassy. He's not really *with* the Embassy; he's just here on a temporary exchange mission to bring Little League Baseball to Brazil. The gal in the flowered dress is his wife." Phil had his other arm around Bert's shoulders, Brazilian style, and he patted Bert's upper arm as he spoke.

"I'd like a drink," Bert said. "Do you want one, Helen?"

"Yes, please, darling."

Phil waved at the butler, who came over immediately with his tray of drinks. "Here. Scotch, gin, or rye? I didn't want to make martinis; it's too hot. But if you want one, I'll sneak you one in the kitchen."

"No, no," said Bert. "Scotch is fine, thank you."

"I found the first Carnival records for fifty-nine," Phil said happily. "I'll play them later and we can dance. Maybe things will get wild."

"Somebody will drop dead of a heat stroke," Mil said. "That's the wild thing that will happen."

"I've got all the windows open," Phil said, beginning to look less happy. "It will get cooler later. Do you want me to bring the fan in from our room?"

"It doesn't do any good in *our* room," Mil said, "so what makes you think it will help with this mob in here?" She walked to the front door to greet other arriving guests, holding her head high, her emerald pendant earrings swinging against her tanned neck.

"She hates the heat," Phil murmured apologetically.

"Don't we all," said Helen. "The front of our apartment is unbearable during the day. I have to stay in the back when I'm home. But at night it's cool."

"It's only the crowd," said Phil. "This is a very cool apartment. Listen, this is Trainer Wilkes. Trainer, Helen and Bert Sinclair."

Trainer Wilkes was a tall, good-looking man in his late thirties. He had curly brown hair and horn-rimmed glasses and a suntan. When he shook hands with Helen he took her hand gently, almost gingerly, as if for years his forceful handshake had made ladies wince and he had finally learned. He was wearing a black silk suit and he looked hot. "How do you do," he said.

"I'm glad to meet you," Helen said. Phil Burns had pulled Bert away to meet someone else, and she found herself alone with Trainer Wilkes. They looked at each other for a minute, trying to think of something to say, and Helen smiled. "Have you been in Brazil long?"

"Few weeks."

"How long are you staying?"

"A year."

"Do you like it? I guess everybody asks you that and you must be sick of hearing it."

"Oh, I like it," Trainer Wilkes said, not too enthusiastically. "Getting to like it. It's interesting. Wouldn't like to live here, but it's all right."

"Where are you from in the States?"

"Garnerville College in Pennsylvania. It's a small school; you've probably never heard of it. But we have one of the best baseball teams in the country."

"I'm afraid I don't know much about baseball," Helen admitted. "My son was too young to play when we left the States. Is that what you do there, teach baseball?" She smiled at him. "I guess that's why they call you 'Trainer.'"

"I teach English history," he said. "English history and baseball."

"And Phil said you're here for the government."

"More or less. I'm with the Cultural Division. We bring our ideas, our culture, over here, and it makes friends. I'm here to teach Little League Baseball. That's my job. And I'll tell you something." He raised his glass and drank thirstily, as if the effort of such a long speech were too much. But his eyes were sparkling and for the first time he looked animated. "It was the best idea they ever had, to bring me over for the Cultural Division. The Brazilians want to know America; let them know baseball. Baseball is *really* America. I don't care about books, music, theater, art, all that junk. I'm going to give 'em baseball, and they're going to love me."

"I hope so," Helen said.

Trainer Wilkes took a clean handkerchief out of his pocket and wiped his face and neck thoroughly, as if it were a hand towel. He looked at it and put it back into his pocket. "You bring your boy over when we get started, and we'll let him join a team," he said. "How old is he?"

"Six. That's a little too young, I think."

"All right. We're going to have a team for five-year-olds. Can't start too young. It must be pretty tough for the American parents here, so far away, trying to keep all the things we have at home."

"But there are certain compensations to travel," Helen said mildly.

Trainer Wilkes looked down into her face seriously. "You be careful," he said. "Just don't get into trouble. You don't know these people."

"What do you mean?"

"You'll know when you get into trouble," Trainer said. "You'll remember I told you."

Someone had put a record of American Christmas carols on the phonograph, and it sounded strange to hear them, almost as if it were really summer and someone were trying to be Bohemian. It was terribly hot. The men were beginning to wipe their foreheads and move closer to the opened windows, and the waiter walked about quickly with ice-filled drinks. The alcohol was only making everyone hotter. "God rest you merry, gentlemen," the chorus sang in wondrously muted harmony. "Let nothing you dismay." It brought memories of Westport in winter, of wreaths hung at windows with sloppily tied red bows attached by Julie, and of the smell of a fir tree and the crackle and heat of a hot fire when you sat too close to it in order to roast apples on long pointed sticks. Lately, more and more often, Helen had been dreaming at night of snow, of wide white fields turning blue at twilight, of windowsills piled high with the powdery fresh snowfall and herself safe inside the room looking out at the white stillness and beauty. All the inconvenience of a Connecticut winter—the icy roads that made driving the children to nursery school a hazard, the biting wind that made you feel you never would get warm again, the ache of wet feet and the beautiful white snow that turned so quickly into brown mud and gray slush—all these things seemed to recede. She remembered winter in Connecticut as if it were a Christmas card.

In the corner of the room on a table was a small Christmas tree, with gold balls and tinsel, and packages underneath it for the Burns's children. Somehow Mil Burns had managed to get real American gift-wrapping paper. Helen recognized it immediately. She had probably sent to the States for the presents, too. There were no other Christmas decorations in the room. Trainer Wilkes had been taken elsewhere by one of the guests, and Helen found herself standing alone. She was relieved. She looked at the other guests idly, noticing their clothes, listening to the Christmas carols with an ache in her throat. She wondered what her friends were doing right now in Westport. It was two hours earlier in the States. They were probably having dinner, or perhaps they were through with dinner and were wrapping last-minute presents furtively, trying to hide them from the excited children. I won't be home again for six Christmases, she thought. Julie will be a teenager. She'll be going to Christmas dances with boys and hanging mistletoe from the top door sill. And I'll be so much older, so much darker skinned, so much blonder, so much a stranger, that all my friends will have to learn to know me all over again, and I them.

She caught sight of Margie standing in a corner talking with two of the American women whom she herself did not know. Margie in her brown and white checked mousseline shirtwaist dress, the skirt propped out by a huge crinoline, looked like a Brazilian wife next to them—chic, pampered, wearing the latest Dior style. The other two women were wearing sunback cotton dresses, the kind Margie wore when she went to the grocery store. They were tanned and contented looking, and they wore a great deal of real gold jewelry set with Brazilian stones. Helen wandered over to them.

"I'll tell you one thing," one was saying in a midwestern accent. "I'm buying a lot of jewelry here. Diamonds especially. Real jewelry is so cheap in Brazil, and it's an investment. Believe me, people treat you better when you have real jewelry. You attract a nicer class of people back home when you have nice jewelry." She held out her hand and looked at her two glittering rings.

Helen tried not to laugh. "That's a lovely aquamarine," she said.

"Isn't it!"

"I'd like you to meet Helen Sinclair," Margie said. "This is—"

"First names," said the woman with the rings. "Ernestine. And this is Linda."

"How do you do," said Linda. She was in her late forties, a small woman, very thin, and she looked shy. Her hair was cut short and curled against her head in tight little snails, as if it had been over-permanented, over-set, and dried too much by the tropical sun. She wore rimless glasses and she had a huge red rubylite hanging around her neck on a gold chain.

"That's a lovely rubylite," Helen said.

"How did you know?" Linda said, smiling happily. "I love it, too; it's my birthstone. My husband gave it to me for my birthday."

"Helen's husband is a gemologist," Margie said. "She knows so much about stones it's terrifying."

"I told her not to stop there," Ernestine said sternly. She gestured at Linda's rubylite pendant. "That's all right, but she should buy *real* stones. Expensive ones. Diamonds."

"I like this one," Linda said.

"You listen to me," said Ernestine. "When you go back to the States you'll be sorry if you haven't bought a few really *good* pieces." She was a big woman, mostly bosom, and she had naturally blond hair which she wore in a ponytail. She looked about thirty-five.

"I'm sure Linda would rather have something her husband gave her for her birthday," Helen said. "I know I would. And this rubylite is a beauty." She smiled at the older woman, feeling sorry for her, and wondering which one of these men was married to Ernestine.

"My birthstone is really garnet," Linda said, in a breathy, rather apologetic voice. "But this is red, so we thought it would count for the same thing."

"Why not?" Margie said.

"Where are you from?" Ernestine asked Helen.

"We lived in Westport, Connecticut, before we came here."

"We've lived all over," Ernestine said. "We lived in California for a while, and in Kansas, and we even lived in Seattle, Washington. Have you ever been there?"

"No, I haven't."

"I like Brazil," Ernestine said. She tossed her head, and the heavy blond pony tail flicked back and forth, rather like the tail of a percheron. When she spoke she showed large, white, even teeth, and she looked like the kind of person who would bite into something to see if it were real. "My husband's going to go into business here. He's thinking of buying land in the jungle and then selling it back in a couple of years when values go up. There's going to be a land boom in the interior when they finish the new capital. It's going to be like the American West, only bigger. Bigger! When they finish the Belém-Brasilia Road, land values out there in the jungle are going to double and redouble."

The butler came by with his tray of highballs and they each took one. "How long have you lived in Brazil?" Helen asked.

"Seven years," Ernestine said. "Let's sit down; my feet hurt." She took hold of Helen's arm and led her to two unoccupied chairs against the wall. "*Ahh* . . . what a relief. You can't get a decent pair of shoes here, especially if you wear an eight and a half triple A. All the Brazilians have little square feet. Did you ever notice?"

"I'd never noticed," Helen said.

"Well, they do. Which one is your husband?"

"That tall man over there," Helen said. "Speaking to the Brazilian."

"Ah, how attractive he is! I love dark men. You're very lucky."

"I think so too," Helen said.

"That handsome one over there on the couch is *my* little boy." Ernestine pointed at a small, balding, rotund man in his early fifties. "He's cute, isn't he?"

Helen would hardly have thought of the word *cute* to describe Ernestine's husband, but she nodded and smiled. "Yes, he is."

Ernestine put her empty highball glass on the floor beside her chair and turned to Helen intimately, her face set in a determined expression of loyalty. She looked like someone about to pledge allegiance to the flag. She twined her fingers around Helen's arm. "Don't sell these people short," Ernestine said.

"These are all wonderful people in this room. Of course, there are a few that are corny—two couples here whose names I won't mention because they won't be here very long. One or two parties and then they'll never be asked back."

"What's *corny*?"

"Wives who flirt too much with other women's husbands. Too much drinking. Acting unrefined. You'll see. Watch any one of the women at this party for half an hour and you'll see that she never does anything out of line. Oh, five, six years ago it was another story. There was lots of carrying on, lots of divorces. But now everyone who comes to Brazil to live has to be screened first by the State Department and they've got rid of all that. All these people here always tread the straight and narrow."

Helen had never actually heard anyone use the expression 'straight and narrow' before. She looked at Ernestine, but Ernestine wore a look of staunch, almost sentimental virtue and not a trace of a smile.

"Let's go over and talk to the men," Ernestine said. She stood up and went over to Bert and the Brazilian, who had been joined by Trainer Wilkes and a tall, thin man Helen did not know.

The men were involved in an excited discussion, and Helen and Ernestine drifted over to the edge of their group without a word, listening politely as people do who are group-hopping at a cocktail party, not sure whether they want to stay or whether they are going to interrupt something highly emotional for the formality of introductions.

Helen wanted to reach out and take Bert's hand or put her arm around his waist. It would make too much of an interruption; she would look like a possessive wife, she was afraid. She always tried to leave him alone at cocktail parties so he would feel free to talk with other people and would not feel that she was his Siamese twin just because she was his wife. After all, they were chained together for good, so they might as well pretend they were free. But she was longing to touch him. She looked at his face, at his lips as he spoke, and she remembered the moment they had had together that evening before all the household things had interrupted. "I'm thinking of something I'm going to do to you tonight."

She could hear his voice inside her head now, saying that again, and she repeated it to herself. The conversation of the men rose and receded around her and she hardly heard it. She was watching her husband, pretending to be interested in the discussion, and she was thinking of the smoothness of his skin under that blue shirt. I can't help it, Helen thought; I want to go home and make love to my husband. I'm bored here and I can't think about anything else except that I want him to make love to me. She wondered if it were the time of the month when she could get pregnant, and if that was why she felt so alive and full of desire. But she felt that way more and more all the time living in Brazil. Perhaps it was the climate. Or perhaps the leisure, or perhaps because the sun and air on the beach made her healthy. I wish it were late and we could go home.

The Doll

Cuti

Not a single one! He was tired from all the walking. He had done a lot of asking and heard all kinds of answers. On some occasions he had reacted to a shop assistant's lack of tact or even to the subtle ironies. On others he had been led to self-commiseration, after hearing, for example:

"I'm so sorry!"

Or:

"You'll forgive us, sir . . . They don't make them, you know?"

Disheartened? No. There was no reason to give up on trying to find a Christmas present for his daughter. He was in great physical shape at 33-years-old. Not only that, it was as if his little girl drove him through the shopping streets. To continue the search, even if trampling over tiredness, was a mission.

Enthusiastically, he entered the next shop. Busy! He waited patiently. A young white girl, with a sweet disposition and a malnourished appearance, inquired:

"Have you been served?"

"No. If you could be so kind, I'm looking for a doll . . . "

"We have loads. Look, here's Barbie, Xuxinha . . . " the blonde girl began to grab various dolls. She set them upon the counter, as if choosing for herself. "Look how cute this one is with its blue eyes. It's new. It arrived yesterday and is almost sold out already. It cries, has a dummy, pees . . . And this other one here, isn't it lovely?" She clutched the fair-skinned yellowy-blonde doll to her chest and moved its little arms and legs around, "Don't you like any of them?"

"The thing is, I'm looking for a black doll . . . "

A half-hour pause.

"We do have some," the store owner said to his employee, "Look better on the shelf below, just up there, by the sink."

The girl went back up the stairs, after smiling in submissive embarrassment.

She came down again, received new instructions and smiled once more. Then, from up on the mezzanine, she waved the chubby, dark brown face of a doll. Beaming, the assistant wielded it like a trophy. She descended the stairs like that, but, careless on the steps, she nosedived. Everyone freaked out. Colleagues rushed to her aid.

Nothing broken. Just a fright. The boss was exasperated, but soon managed to collect himself, red as a chili pepper. The shop was full. He went to deal with the customer.

"Excuse the delay and the commotion, sir, but it was nothing. The important thing is we found the product. It's low in stock, you know? . . . They don't send them. I ordered some myself last week, but the representative said the company was exporting to Africa. That's fine, but there's customers here looking for them, too, aren't there? Are you Brazilian, sir?"

"Yes."

"Well . . . " He swallowed his sentence and prepared the receipt.

Out in the street, the father, among other thoughts, some of them unsavory, figured that some relaxation was called for after sweating out expectations on that December morning. He took a deep breath. He looked around at the beautiful arrangements of Christmas decorations, dominated by Santa Claus, blonde children, and lots of snow. He carried on, walking slowly, toward a bar.

"A cold blonde one, buddy?" Asked the barman, seeing him settle into a stool.

He smiled and gave a thumbs up.

With the first gulp of beer, he felt profoundly relieved and happy.

A Christmas Story

Luiz Ruffato

A TRUE STORY THAT HAPPENED IN THE DAYS WHEN ANIMALS TALKED AND READ THE NEWSPAPER, AND NEWSPAPERS INFLUENCED PUBLIC OPINION.

This is a story from the days when animals could talk.

Back then there were still newspapers. They were read and talked about, they influenced public opinion—and almost all of them had literary supplements, can you believe it, dear reader? The periodicals (which is another way we can refer to newspapers) of the big cities had enormous newsrooms and huge printing presses that employed hundreds of people and were widely circulated. And so the delivery trucks, which left the city for the interior in the early morning, also served as a kind of private couriers, carrying mail quickly back and forth. Many of these periodicals relied on correspondents in cities in the interior and, in the most important ones, they were able to maintain branch offices with a set number of journalists.

Well. One day, the bureau chief of a branch office—let's call him Tanganelli (if you don't like the name, you can use another, no problem)—called the head of the transport department (the person responsible for the delivery trucks) and said:

—Silveira (ditto, if you don't like the name), it's Tanganelli from the Ribeirão Preto office (you can change the city name too!). Here's the thing: I asked a cousin of mine to buy my kids' presents there in São Paulo, it's much cheaper, and I suddenly thought, if he dropped the package off there, maybe you could send it to me . . . It's a small package, it won't be a bother . . .

I should mention that this story takes place the week of Christmas—a Monday, with the 25th falling on Saturday—and Silveira was feeling particularly empathetic because his pregnant wife was about to give birth at any moment.

Silveira told Tanganelli that it wouldn't be a problem at all, that he could tell his cousin to look for him, or, if he couldn't find Silveira, to leave the parcel for him, and he would send it out that night. Having said this, Silveira got to work on his daily tasks, which consisted of signing documents, verifying the accounts of the trucks entering and leaving, attending long, useless meetings—and he was still able to keep abreast of progress of his wife's condition. At four in the afternoon, Marcão relieved him, and he got in his car and drove home, happy to have accomplished another day's duties.

On Tuesday, half an hour after arriving at work, the phone on his desk rang, and Silveira picked up. It was Tanganelli asking if he had received the package that his cousin had left the day before. He answered that, since it hadn't been during his shift, someone else must have received it and held on to it, but not to worry, next morning the parcel would be in his hands. Tanganelli thanked him, very happy, and hung up.

Silveira called the errand boy, instructed him to find the package and put it in the cabinet, he'd take care of it later, then immersed himself in his routine. At four o'clock on the dot, Marcão arrived, they exchanged pleasantries, and Silveira left. He was already on the road when he remembered the package and, annoyed, promised himself that as soon as he set foot in his house he'd call his colleague and ask him to arrange for the package to be sent to Ribeirão Preto. But, as you know, reader, the traffic in São Paulo is terrible. Silveira lived far away in a rented apartment, airy and sun-filled, but far, and, upon parking the car in the garage, his only thought was of hugging his wife and feeling their baby's little feet kicking in her belly, a heart-warming thing.

On Wednesday, still in the hallway, Silveira heard the telephone ringing shrilly and immediately remembered about Tanganelli. Flustered, he opened the locker, checked that the package was there, and only then picked up the phone. On the other end was Tanganelli sounding extremely irritated, but restrained:

—Hello, Silveira, nothing arrived here for me!

Sheepish, Silveira said:

—I'm sorry, Tanganelli . . . My wife is pregnant, and at this time of year problems pile up . . . I'm mortified, I'm so very sorry. But look, by the end of the day, I guarantee . . .

Hanging up the phone, Silveira thought about how to remember to take the package to Normando, the subordinate who was in charge of dispatching the trucks to the interior, and who started work at the same time Silveira left. At first, he planned to place the package on top of his desk, but because the box was light and fragile, he was afraid he might knock it off, break something, no, it was better not to risk it. Upon reflection, he took a piece of paper and wrote in bold letters, with a Pilot pen, "Package for Riberão Preto" and Scotch-taped it to the door of the cabinet.

The morning flew by, as they say. After lunch, they gathered for an interminable meeting to discuss the details of the staff Christmas party–on Saturday morning, Santa would arrive in a helicopter in the company courtyard and distribute presents to the children. Returning to his office, Silveira found he had so many things to finish that, even though he looked at the sign on the locker door now and then, he only realized he hadn't sent Tangenelli's package when he woke, alarmed, in front of television, in the wee hours of the morning.

On Thursday, still on his way to work, it seemed like he could already hear the racket of the telephone that followed him until he entered the office. As soon as he sat down and picked up the device, he heard, on the other end, Tanganelli's shouts. Not knowing what to say, Silveira, who was a good man, merely murmured, You're completely right, I don't know what to say, It'll be sent today, without fail, etc.

Silveira managed the morning badly. He placed the package in plain sight, on the desk, and looked at his watch every hour, anxious for four o'clock to arrive so he could take the package to Normando. But shortly after lunch, he got a phone call from his neighbor telling him to come running home, his wife was complaining that she wasn't feeling well. He phoned Marcão, and his colleague agreed to come in earlier, not to worry, in half an hour, forty minutes max, he would be there, Silveira could go calmly. Silveira left the office early, and en route, remembered, annoyed, Tanganelli's damned package . . . What a pain! He arrived, panting, at home and, after verifying that his wife was feeling better, called Marcão. He told him about Tanganelli, leaving out the unnecessary details of course, and asked him to let Normando know to send the package to Ribeirão Preto, without fail, do you hear?

As soon as he put the phone back on the hook, Marcão was absorbed into his routine. It was already almost midnight, the end of his shift, when, seeing the package on the desk, he remembered Silveira's words. He phoned Normando immediately, telling him he had a package in his office that had to be sent that day, without fail, do you hear, to Ribeirão Preto. Normando told him not to worry, that he would put it on the first truck leaving for the interior. Marcão turned out the lights, closed the office door, and notified the guard that someone would stop by later to pick up the merchandise.

About forty minutes later, a truck approached the door of the transport department. The guard accompanied the boy to the department head's office, opened the door, and turned on the lights. They saw the sign stuck to the door of the cabinet, "Package for Ribeirão Preto."

The next day, Silveira almost had a heart attack upon seeing Tanganelli's damned package undisturbed on top of his desk. The only person who was more surprised was Tanganelli who, arriving at the small office where the branch was located, came upon the three journalists and the secretary who worked with him looking baffled at the sight of the old cabinet that had just arrived from the headquarters in São Paulo.

My Christmas

Clarice Lispector

When the children were too small to stay awake for a midnight supper on Christmas Eve, we would celebrate Christmas over lunch the following day. The children grew up, but the custom remained. And we always exchange presents on the morning of the 25th.

Since our Christmas meal was on the 25th, I was always free on Christmas Eve. However, for the last three or four years, I have had a sacred rendezvous for the night of the 24th.

I was talking to a young woman who was not my friend at the time, but who now is, and a very dear one too, and I asked what she was planning to do on Christmas Eve and who she was going to spend it with. She replied very simply: the same thing I do every year: I take some pills that send me to sleep for forty-eight hours. I was surprised, not to say alarmed, and I asked her why. It turns out that she found Christmas a particularly painful festival, because she had, I understand, lost both her parents around that time of year, and could not bear to spend Christmas without them. I pointed out how dangerous those pills could be: instead of sending her to sleep for forty-eight hours, they might put her to sleep for good.

I had an idea: from then on, we would spend part of Christmas Eve together, having supper in a restaurant. We would meet at around eight o'clock, and she would see then how packed the restaurants were with other people who have no home or no homely atmosphere where they can spend Christmas and who, therefore, choose to celebrate it elsewhere. After supper, she drops me off at my place and then goes home to pick up her aunt so that they can attend Midnight Mass together. We agreed that we would each pay for our own supper and would exchange presents, which was our being there for each other.

One Christmas, though, my friend was unable to keep our appointment, and, even though she knew I was not religious, she gave me a missal. I opened it, and in it she had written: pray for me.

In September of the following year, a fire broke out in my bedroom, a fire that left me so badly burned that, for some days, my life hung in the balance. My room was completely destroyed: the plaster on the walls and the ceiling fell in, the furniture was reduced to ashes, as were my books.

I won't even attempt to explain what happened: everything was destroyed, but the missal remained intact, apart from a little singeing on the cover.

Second Pang

Alphonsus de Guimaraens

. . . Angelus Domini apparuit in somnis Joseph . . .
Qui consurgens accepit puerum et matrem ejus
nocte, et seccessit in Aegyptum.

S. MATTH. II, 13, 14.

-I-

There were rough shepherds and shepherdesses
That at the softness of dawn's clear light
Are by the Eastern sun blushed with kisses,
And transform into visions of delight:

And gentle and mild, hands joined in prayer,
Were bands of fair-haired children, and the old,
Of humble aspect, dreaming souls laid bare,
Where the blessing of the Lord unfolds.

It was the sublime worship of the throng,
In the Creche's heavenly glow,
Before the berth of the boy so young:

Before the berth in which he lay,
Flower-bedecked today, enshrouded tomorrow,
Cradle of God, but Holy Tomb one day.

- II -

Of mighty radiance was the immense star
That led them to the Holy Place through desert night . . .
Myrrh Balthazar carried: incense, Gaspar:
Melchior, gold that gleams so bright.

There were valleys and hills, and woods so dense
And the field spread out in mantle verdant:
And in the moonlight, all jasper, and under sun intense,
They followed on the wing of divine enchantment.

When under the same roof they came in good hour
Where the immaculate Family had sought shelter,
In their Souls bloomed ethereal Affection's flower.

And the Magi, with gaze humble and gentle,
Their Diadems they doffed, dust and nothing,
Before He who was the Word eternal.

- III -

The three Magis' sacred adoration,
At the feet of Christ genuflection pious,
What clouds you augur, what divinations,
Winds that brought you to the Home so precious!

Your affections' singular cries,
And the same prayer today, of my contrition,
Make in the Tetrarch vague hate arise . . .
And afterwards, arrived Anguish and affliction.

Thou wilt go, Lady, to the scorching lands
Where the great Pyramid, unadorned,
The steps of swift time stops and holds.

Turn to Him, slowly, eyes in lamentation:
Leave Judea behind, as it reveals to you, dear Lady,
The Kings of the East's strange adoration.

- IV -

Joseph, the Carpenter, son of Kings,
From the House of the Psalmist descended,
Awakens in darkest night, his body shaking,
His sight by strike of lightning rended.

With a warrior's semblance, a Cherub blazing white
Adorned with conqueror's sable heraldry,
From darkness mixed with radiant light,
It surges from gray clouds all misty.

On a pentacle of stars was writ:
"Make welcome, Husband, the Son of God,
To the burning sands of Egypt."

"My God!" exclaims the Saint, and mutely spies
The bright Archangel's golden face:
A fount of tears springs from his eyes.

- V -

The donkey opens kindhearted eyes,
And traverses mountains and gullies.
And the Mother, distressed, with the Husband, just alive,
The couple all in anguish hurries.

The hours of dread and the agonizing
Days, Lo: the Pain commences early.
In the darkness surge specters now revived:
And unceasing is the nightmare's tragedy.

Then follow clear days, stifling nights,
And the heavens, a turquoise of full moonlight,
Cloud over with sorrow, tears and sighs.

And one seems to hear the steps so gentle
Of the moon, poor and lifeless, wand'ring
In cold space's hieratic castles.

- VI -

Hands that are the lilies' envy, hands elect
To relieve of his suffering the blessed Christ,
Whose veins of blue seem constructed
Of the same astral essence as the blessed eyes:

Hands of dreaming and belief, hands adept
To guide the slow steps of the one dying,
And in centuries of faith, roses stripp't
In hymns above convent towers sighing:

Hands the holy Scapular sewing,
That Thou revealed, the Rosary:
Ineffable comfort to the suffering.

Hands anointed in the blood of the Crown,
Let on my praying Soul cascade
The blessing that redeems us as His own!

- VII -

For the unhappy, sweet consolation,
First and last support to those who weep,
Oh! Give to me scars, give to me restoration,
For the wounds I now present to Thee.

Give me happy hours, days of light,
The innocence of mornings of olden days:
The clouds on which your steps alight
Transform at dawn to golden rays.

Thou that art among the thorns white Rose,
Guiding star at high seas, strong-tower tall,
Come, dear Lady, and right paths to me expose.

When I meditate on your Seven Sorrows,
I in my soul the pain of death can feel
Of all my sins and all my horrors . . .

Pax Domestica

Victor Heringer

H*iiii! Good morning, good morning, good morning, good morning!*

Great, great, and yours?

Yes, I went. I couldn't not, could I. Or my mother would have disowned me. My family, my mother, she loves Christmas. I told you, didn't I: every year, in November, she throws away all the decorations and buys new ones. Glass baubles, miniature Father Christmases, styrofoam snow. All new. To renew life. Throw everything away, buy it all again.

I don't much like this woman. Her voice is nasally and shrill, but when she laughs the air comes out in a cough, all through her mouth. A happy bray. She's going to tell me she travelled to Mato Grosso, where her mother lives. *My mother and father. And the whole gang of cousins! (Laughs)* Somewhere in the middle of nowhere, fewer than 10,000 inhabitants, a ranch satellite town. Cattle and soy, cattle and soy. She's going to tell me what the journey was like: she forgot her headphones. She had to travel in silence for nine hours, the bus left Belo Horizonte in the afternoon and got to Mato Grosso at night. On Christmas Eve itself. *Not even a radio, imagine, not even a little radio!* She'll try to describe the scenery, that green, brown, dull gold sameness. The electricity poles marking the speed of the bus; the wires going dooown, the wires going uuup, up and down, up and down. Further back, the grasslands going by slowly, and even further back, the hills going by even more slowly. When night fell the road went into the mountains and she saw the moon and the stars twirling: bend to the left, bend to the right. She'll try and explain: the whole scene moving at different speeds and in different directions, like a puppet show. This comparison will sprout from the sludge in her head, it wants to float up to the light, but it's no use. The jolts in perspective have left her confused.

Daddy picked her up from the bus station.

Who was at the house? Were they all there already?

"Me, your mother, grandpa, Auntie Sá, your cousin and her boyfriend . . ."

How am I meant to know which cousin? It was cousin Marô, with her boyfriend, who she'd brought to meet the family. *So it's getting serious.* Next there'll be a wedding, which this woman calls 'getting hitched' because she's just back from the sticks.

"Serious, oh yes."

What was he like?

"He doesn't like music."

What?

"Says he doesn't like it. It disturbs him."

Daddy drove, giving her a smile every now and again, neither of them talking. As soon as they went through the gates, he took a deep breath and said:

"There'll be an empty seat at the table."

In previous years, there'd been no end of family. They'd had to improvise, more tables, deckchairs, benches, mummy sitting on a pouffe, joyfulness unbridled.

It seemed the cousin had changed too.

"You know your cousin likes to read, don't you. So your mother started telling her she was reading a book about that guy who invented the iPod. You know what your cousin said? That nobody reads that kind of book, a book about the guy who invented the iPod, she'd never be capable of inventing the iPod. That she'd thrown her money away. That a book like that was just to take money from people like her. Not that your mother is going to invent the iPod, but . . ."

SNOW IS CHIC

The dogs of the house greeted her. Two Fila Brasileiros, muscular, half-feral. Not those little dogs rich women have, with bows and no fleas, no ticks. These dogs had cayenne ticks, horse ticks! They'd get them out in the scrub. Rodolfo and Maguila, their names were. After that, the whole family: yay. *I love my family.* (Don't I.)

The boyfriend was the last in the queue for hugs. A big guy with a fat neck, a goatee and a gormless smile. The strong fat type – *you know the strong fat type?* – and pretty ugly. The cousin, she was no beauty, one of those teachers who think they don't need to make more than three thousand reais a month, one of those women who think they don't need to shave their armpits, but shave them anyway. The cousin, she'd do better for herself if she learned a few make up tips and went out dancing and was more persistent and prayed to Saint Anthony. You can get tutorials for anything on the internet. A kiss on the cheek: hi, pleased to meet you, and the boyfriend said his name. She said hers. Pleased to meet you.

Mummy! They hug again.

Christmas dinner is already on the table, awaiting her arrival.

On the stereo, Sinatra singing jingle bells.

The father always sits at the head of the table, with the mother on his right and the daughter on his left. Beside the daughter, cousin Marô. Opposite the cousin, an empty chair, though the place is set with a plate and cutlery. Beside the empty place, the boyfriend. Why didn't he sit in front of his girlfriend? I don't know, I don't care. Opposite him, Auntie Sá. At the other end of the table, the patriarch, the father's father, grandpa, staring with curiosity and rage at the new intruder, a hunk of flesh twice his size and a quarter of his age.

The plates and cups and saucers are Chinese, from when China still sold expensive things. The cutlery actual silver. On the glass serving dishes: roast turkey; a Chester super-chicken in apricot sauce; ham glazed with honey, pineapple and cloves; cod with boiled potatoes and red, green and yellow peppers. Bowls of: caramelized fruit; dried fruit; rice with raisins; banana farofa. Full-fat desserts: crème caramel; panettone; dulce de leche; cheese and guava; coconut brittle and Grace Kelly cakes, a family tradition.

This year's decorations: a Christmas tree with white plastic foliage, even whiter plastic imitation snow on top. Gold glitter. Gold glass baubles hanging from the branches. A Star of David, gold, fixed to the top of the tree. Gold ornaments stuck on the walls, Father Christmases in white and gold woolly hats, white reindeer, the words HAVE A MERRY SNOWY CHRISTMAS! in English. The temperature: 36°C.

"Snow is chic," says the mother.

The boyfriend gives a low, mocking cough.

MOTHER: I change the decorations every year.

The boyfriend smiles, doesn't answer. She's not his mother-in-law, he doesn't have to answer.

GRANDPA: (*loudly*) She changes them every year.

The boyfriend smiles at the old man. Silence.

Everybody starts talking at the same time. Their voices swell and soften. Silence. Daddy starts cutting the ham. Grandpa sticks his fork in the turkey. Is there no pork shoulder? Auntie Sá asks about boyfriends. *Every auntie asks the same thing, don't they.* (*Laughs*). Someone asks for the rice to be passed. Ah . . . boyfriends, nothing, or almost nothing. A few wimps, boys, no assertiveness; all poodle. A woman wants a Fila Brasileiro, a Labrador. *Not one of those pit bull types from the gym, mind you, none of that. Nor a Rottweiler, not that either.* A brute, pero no mucho.

Every day on her way home from work, she passes a jiu-jitsu gym (DODÔ FIGHT). From the street, she sees the tough guys grappling on the floor – men, those stocky women and, sometimes, a scared-looking fat kid (dad's idea, put the boy in a fight). From the street, she smells sweat mixed with tatami, the reek of man and rubber that she adores, that frightens her, that gives her goosebumps, a man like that turns me to jelly. And if you could have the smell without the man, how good would that be! There's no prince charming without the smell of tatami.

GRANDPA: (*Loudly*) Did you bring a present?

FATHER: He doesn't need to bring a present.

GRANDPA: (*Loudly*) It would be polite.

AUNTIE SÁ: He can join our Secret Santa.

The boyfriend says nothing.

COUSIN MARÔ: He's going to play charades.

MOTHER: Nobody needs to bring a present. Pass the turkey?

CUIABÁ IS NOT CHIC

MOTHER: Doesn't he remind you of someone?

AUNTIE SÁ: He does, doesn't he?

FATHER: Of who?

(The father realises who. His face goes as red as a pepper.)

AUNTIE SÁ: He really does . . .

FATHER: I'm going to the bathroom. Excuse me.

MOTHER: Napkin. Wipe your mouth.

He wipes his mouth. Visibly upset. And exits. White cloth napkin with gold hems, brand new, thirty-five reais each.

MOTHER: (*To the boyfriend*) Do you like the decorations?

DAUGHTER: (*Jokey voice*) She changes them every year.

Nobody laughs.

The boy nods.

AUNTIE SÁ: There really is a resemblance. What's your father's name?

The boy answers.

The mother and the aunt whisper.

GRANDPA: (*Loudly*) What?

AUNTIE SÁ: He isn't from Cuiabá.

MOTHER: Where are you from?

AUNTIE SÁ: Pass the turkey?

The boyfriend doesn't say where he's from.

AUNTIE SÁ: Do you remember?

MOTHER: The past is past. Over and done. Pass the cod.

GRANDPA: (*Loudly*) Is there no pork shoulder?

Everyone falls silent, passing plates and serving dishes to one another, until the father comes back from the bathroom. He sits and wipes his mouth with the napkin, slowly, almost voluptuously. A clean mouth is a very pleasant thing. Daddy is clean, daddy never did anyone any harm. Faithful to God.

FATHER: Zaga cut his leg. Looked deep.

MOTHER: (*Explaining to the audience*) Zaga is the caretaker.

GRANDPA: (*Loudly*) He knows how to turn his eyelids inside out so you only see the fleshy side. Like an animal. His wife has hepatitis. Hepatitis A or B.

FATHER: Or C.

GRANDPA: (*Loudly*) What?

BOYFRIEND: Hepatitis est omnis divisa in partes tres.

An astonished silence followed his words. It must have been funny.

GRANDPA: (*Loudly*) What?

The boyfriend smiles, but doesn't answer. He doesn't repeat or explain the joke. Not even cousin Marô understood what he was trying to say.

GRANDPA: (*Loudly*) Son, who did you vote for president?

FATHER: You don't have to answer.

MOTHER: I really like this year's decorations. I chose them. Don't you like them? It's a shame to throw them all away afterwards. But we have to renew.

The boy doesn't answer. He gives an odd smile.

Then, you won't believe what happened. He sniffed the air like a dog and got up from the table, my cousin's boyfriend. He looked like he was possessed. Everyone stood up, as though overcome by a profound solemnity. *Then he turned his back and walked towards the stairs. Everyone followed, including me, even now I can't say why.* It was like a funeral procession. Then they realised there was no music playing. Not a single jingle bell. The sound of footsteps going after the boy. Stairs. Someone helped Grandpa climb them. The boy went towards a room that nobody ever opened. It was like he already knew. *When mummy realised where we were going, she stood still, watching.* Watching her family leave. Her daughter beckoned her to follow, even though she didn't know where she was going. The mother remained impassive, panic-struck.

The boy turned the handle, but the door was locked. *Everyone looked at my mother, didn't they, she has all the keys to the house.* But the mother didn't react at all. Everything was about to fall apart. Then the boy kicked the door once, twice. The lock held. *So then my father, my father seemed hypnotised, he went over and broke down the door with one shove of his shoulder.* Inside, there were dozens of cardboard boxes stacked on top of each other.

You'll never believe what was in the boxes.

The decorations from all the Christmases before.

The Atheist

Rachel de Queiroz

Once upon a time, long ago, there was a man who was an atheist. In the little village where he lived, there was no one else who was an atheist like him, so the poor man lived in great isolation. But he was proud and didn't complain, even when he felt especially lonely, like on Sundays when everyone would attend Mass and he went on wandering among the trees in the square; or on Christmas Eve, when everyone was concerned only with the Nativity and Midnight Mass. They set off fireworks, the bells tolled, and everyone rejoiced and went to eat dinner, but the atheist declined their invitations: not having prayed, he didn't think he had a right to supper, for though he was an atheist, he was honest; he shut himself up in his house and read one of his books about atheism by candlelight. And, if one of the people who had come a long way to join in the village festivities was surprised by the silhouette of a lone man reading in the cool breeze of his window and asked why he wasn't at Mass or at Christmas dinner, the villagers explained:

—He can't, the poor thing. He's our atheist.

Otherwise, the atheist lived like everyone else. He labored at his trade, planted cabbage and oregano in the garden, raised two hunting dogs, and, at nightfall, he joined the group of his fellow countrymen who sat talking on the steps of the fountain. And when the conversation touched on the subject of religion someone would always remark:

—You, since you're an atheist . . .

They didn't say this to offend him, but simply because it was true; in reality, they all regarded him highly since, though an atheist, he was a good atheist.

But the year came when our atheist, for various reasons, seemed to start feeling even more lonely. I forgot to mention that he was a bachelor. Although the city took a certain degree of pride in possessing such a rarity—a declared atheist—the young ladies didn't have the courage to marry a man so marked and who, no sooner than he was deceased, would be directed straight to hell.

A canine disease came and killed the two hunting dogs; it seemed like a punishment to further deepen the poor atheist's solitude. And his books, read over and over again, had nothing left to tell him. During the day, work helped to keep him occupied; and in the afternoon, he saw some friends. But in those days, people were very religious, and they spent a lot of time in church: there was Mass in the morning, rosary in the afternoon, novena at night, and for every little holiday, processions. And in those many hours when everyone was in church, the atheist left his house, sat in the shade of the crucifix, smelled the pleasant scent of incense burning in the thuribles, which gave him a certain urge to go in, to see the gold on the saints' robes, and listen to the priest's beautiful Latin. But he restrained himself; what would the people say if they saw him there in the church?

There were other occasions for envy on procession days, when all his friends dressed in colorful silk robes and carried the bier, the poles of the processional canopy, or the great, flaming torches, and he stood on the street corner, his hands hanging from his elbows, in his old everyday clothes. And so he would go back to work, even though it was a feast day, and no one was scandalized by it because they all understood that he was an atheist, though they lamented his misfortune.

And it was then, at the end of that year, that a young lady—the priest's niece as it happens—fell in love with the atheist. How it began, no one knows, but that's how love is: a young woman walks down the street, spots a man she's seen all her life, and suddenly feels a thud in her chest and falls in love with him.

At first he felt merely the warmth of her glances, so sweet and friendly; but after, discovering that he was loved—he, who no one loved—he began to love her as well.

And everyone in the village felt sorry for the lovers, knowing they couldn't think of getting married, that the priest wouldn't hand over his innocent little lamb to a confessed atheist.

And so Christmas arrived and the Nativity was set up and the pilgrimage of visitors coming to kiss the foot of the Baby Jesus began. And the atheist's lover insisted that he accompany her on this obligatory visit. He said no and only after great difficulty would he consent to enter the room and remain in a corner, while she performed her devotions. But this the young woman would not accept:

—How much does a kiss cost? Don't you kiss me?

He smiled:

—But you are a person of flesh and blood, and I love you. The Baby Jesus, as you call him, is a little china doll.

The young woman argued that the cup he lifted to his lips was also made of china and it had never done him any harm. So he pleaded on the basis of his pride. After all, he was the local atheist, the only one. At this point, the girl began to cry, saying that if he loved himself more than he loved her, it was all over. The atheist was frightened by the threat and agreed, though he was ashamed. He accompanied the triumphant young woman, got in line behind her, encountering looks of astonishment. One by one, the devout stopped in front of the manger, bent a knee, prayed fervently, and kissed the foot of the Baby Jesus. His lover's turn arrived and, having venerated the Baby Jesus and given it a kiss, turned around and smiled at the good atheist, encouraging him. He looked about him and saw the same look of exhilaration and hope on every face. He was resolved: he bent his rough knee, bowed his head over the tiny feet of the saint. And under his lips he felt, not the cold of porcelain, but the heat of flesh; the movement, the pulse of flesh. He raised his eyes, terrified. He gazed at the Baby Jesus and saw He was smiling radiantly, and from his eyes shone a light that eyes of china would never have.

They say the atheist fell to the ground, with his arms crossed, crying and worshiping. And that Christmas night saw the end of the village's only atheist.

But they also say that he didn't marry his lover. He couldn't. Instead, he abandoned everything and became a monk.

Christmas Turkey

Mário de Andrade

Our first family Christmas after my father's death, five months earlier, had decisive consequences for the familial happiness. We had always been familiarly happy, in that most abstract sense of the word: decent people, no crimes, no domestic quarrels or serious financial hardship. But, due largely to the gray nature of my father, a being entirely devoid of poetry, possessed of an impeccable incompetence and swaddled in mediocrity, we'd lacked a certain enjoyment of life, a taste for material pleasures, a good wine, an outing to the hot springs, the purchase of a refrigerator, that sort of thing. My father had been a good man of the worst sort, dramatically so; he was a purebred killjoy.

My father died, we were terribly sorry, etc. By the time we were approaching the Christmas season, I was about done with the obstructive memory of the dead man, which seemed to have inculcated for all time the need for mournful tribute at every lunch, at every turn in the family's life. Once I suggested to Mom that she might go to the theater, to see a movie, which only led to tears. How would that look, deep in mourning, and going to see a movie! Grief was being kept up for the sake of appearances, and I, whose affection for my father had been average at best, a son's instinct more than any spontaneous outpouring of love, was beginning to feel I'd had it with the very good man.

It was certainly from this that sprang—quite spontaneously, this time—the idea of getting up to one of my so-called "high-jinks." That had been, in fact, from very early on, my most splendid triumph over the environment at home.

Since my high school days, when I could be counted on to fail a class every year; since I stole a kiss from a cousin, at the age of ten, and was found out by Tia Velha, my abominable elderly aunt, and especially since the lessons I took (or gave, who knows) involving the maid of some relatives: I managed to get, in the reformatory that was my home and among our vast relations, the conciliatory reputation of being "crazy." "He's crazy, poor thing!" they'd say. My parents said it with a certain condescending resignation, the rest of the relatives as a lesson to hold over their kids, and probably with the particular pleasure that comes with being convinced of their own superiority. None of their children were crazy. It was what saved me, that reputation. I took advantage of everything life offered me and that was essential to becoming more fully myself. And they let me get away with it all—because I was crazy, poor thing. This afforded me an existence without complexes, and I can't complain one bit.

It had always been a tradition in the family, Christmas dinner. A lousy dinner, as you can imagine: my father's type of thing, chestnuts, figs, raisins, after Midnight Mass. Stuffed full of walnuts and almonds (how we argued, we three kids, over the nutcracker . . .), full of chestnuts and boredom, we'd hug each other and head to bed. Thinking back on all that, I burst out with one of my "high jinks":

—Okay, on Christmas, I want to eat turkey.

The kerfuffle this caused, you can't imagine. My aunt, a pious old maid who lived with us, was quick to note that we couldn't possibly invite anyone over because we were in mourning.

—But who said anything about inviting anyone! It's always the same damn thing . . . When have we been able to eat turkey in this house! Turkey is only for parties, when all those damn relatives come over . . .

—Please don't talk that way, my dear . . .

—I'll talk however I want, and that's that!

I unleashed on them my icy disdain for our endless stream of relatives, supposedly descended from the first explorers, as if I care! It was just the moment to elaborate on my theory of being crazy, poor thing, I wasn't going to miss the chance. I was struck by an immense love for my mom and my auntie, my two mothers, three if you include my sister—the three mothers who have always graced my life. It was the same old story: someone's birthday would come along, and only then they'd make turkey. Turkey was for special occasions, when a filthy horde of relations, well-trained by tradition, would mount an invasion, all of them after the turkey, the little pies, the sweets. My three mothers would've done nothing but work for three days making the finest, most elaborate deserts and cold cuts, the swarm of relatives would devour everything and even wrap up what was left to take home to anyone who hadn't made it. My three mothers were left beside themselves with exhaustion. Of the turkey, mom and aunty would only taste what could be picked off the bones the next day at Christmas lunch, some vague, dark bit of thigh, lost in the white, white rice. And that's what Mom would serve, picking out all she could for her old man and the children. Truth was, no one really knew what turkey was in our house, table scrap turkey.

So no, we weren't going to invite anyone. It would be a turkey for us, for the five of us. And there would be two types of farofa, a rich one heaping with giblets, and the other fluffy and golden, with lots of butter. We'd stuff the bird with the rich one, and to that we'd add prunes, walnuts and a glass of sherry, like I'd learned from my best girl, Rose. Of course, I never mentioned where I picked up the recipe, but everyone had their suspicions. They all looked a bit ruffled, wondering if such a delicious recipe might not be a trap laid by the Wicked One himself. And cold beer too, I declared, at the top of my voice. The truth is that my own tastes, grown rather refined away from home, called for a good wine, entirely French. But affection for Mom beat out the crazy in me, and Mom loved beer.

After I laid out my plans, I could see everyone was ecstatic, dying to get on with the craziness I'd proposed. They knew well enough that yes, this was insane, but they managed to believe that I was the one who really wanted it and could easily lay on me the guilt they felt for their wayward desires. They smiled and exchanged glances, timid as doves, until my sister said what they were all thinking:

—He's crazy all right!

The turkey was purchased, prepared, etc. And after some pretty distracted praying during Midnight Mass, we had our most wonderful Christmas of all. It was a funny thing: those days, whenever I remembered that I was finally going to get Mom to eat turkey, I'd be overcome with thoughts of her, full of affection and love for my dear old lady. And my siblings, too, were taken with the same violent outburst of love, all swept up in this newfound happiness that the turkey stirred in the family. So, to cover things up a bit, I sat back calmy and let Mom carve the whole turkey breast. At a certain point, in fact, she stopped, having carved one side into slices, giving in to the laws of thrift that had long lulled her into a near-destitution that made no sense.

—No, ma'am, cut the whole thing! I'd eat all that on my own!

It wasn't true. Familial love was burning so brightly in me that I might even have gone as far as to eat very little, just so's the other four could eat too much. And we were all in tune on this. Eating that turkey made just for us renewed in each one the tenderness, the love—a mother's love, a child's love—that had been smothered by routine. Lord help me, I even thought of Jesus . . . In that home of the very modestly bourgeois, a miracle was taking place that was worthy of the birth of a God. The turkey breast was now entirely reduced to thick slices.

—I'll serve!

"He's really crazy," because why ever would I serve the food, when Mom had always served it in this house! Laughing, they passed the big heaping plates along to me and I began the heroic distribution, telling my brother to pour the beer. Right away I took a choice piece of crispy skin, rich and juicy, and put it on a plate. Then some great big slices of white meat. Mom's voice rose reproachful and cut through the anguish with which everyone longed for a piece of that turkey.

—Remember your siblings, Juca!

How could she have guessed, poor dear, that this plate was for her—for Mother, my neglected friend, who knew about Rose, who knew about my mischief, who I only ever remembered to tell things that made her suffer! The plate was magnificent.

—Mom, this one's for you! No! No, don't pass it on!

That was when, beside herself with all the commotion, she began to cry. My aunt, realizing that the next outrageous serving would be hers, joined the tearful chorus. And my sister, who never saw a tear without turning on the faucet herself, began to bawl. I started to spout all sorts of nonsense so's not to cry myself, I was nineteen years old . . . Damn family that can't see a turkey without bursting into tears! that sort of thing. Everyone tried hard to keep smiling, but by this point, any happiness was beyond our reach. All the weeping had conjured, by association, the unwelcome image of my dead father. Cutting a gray figure as usual, he had come to ruin our Christmas once and for all, and I was fuming.

So we started to eat, quietly, mournfully, and the turkey was perfect. The tame flesh, of tenderest texture, floated delightfully between the farofas and the ham, bruised at times, riled up and reinvigorated, by the rather violent intervention of a prune or the impertinent disruption of little bits of walnut. But Dad sat there, enormous and imprecise, a reprobation, a wound, an incapacity. And the turkey, so delicious, finally letting mom known why it was a delicacy truly worthy of the newborn baby Jesus.

A silent struggle broke out between the turkey and Dad's hulking figure. I thought praising the turkey would strengthen it—because, obviously, I'd very much taken the turkey's side. But the dead have their sticky, hypocritical ways of winning: as soon as I opened my mouth to compliment the turkey, Dad's image grew, victorious and unbearably obstructionist.

—If only your father were here . . .

I was so focused on the struggle between the dead pair that I couldn't eat, couldn't even enjoy that perfect turkey. I came to hate Dad. In a burst of inspiration coming from who knows where, I turned phony and diplomatic. In that moment, which now seems to have been decisive for our family, I gave the impression of taking my father's side. Forlorn, I put on a front:

—It's true . . . But Dad, who loved us so much, who died working for our sakes, Dad up in heaven must be so happy . . . (I hesitated, then decided not to mention the turkey) . . . so happy to see all of us, here, together as a family.

And very calmy, everyone started talking about Dad. His image shrank and shrank, until it turned into a bright little star in the sky. Now everyone ate the turkey with relish, because Dad had been so good, he'd sacrificed so much for us, he was a saint: "You, my children, will never be able to repay what you owe your father." A saint. Dad had become a saint, a comforting contemplation, the merest little star in the sky. And as a pure object of serene contemplation, he bothered no one. The only dead one left was the turkey, commanding and entirely victorious.

My mother, my aunt, all of us were overflowing with happiness. I was going to write "overstuffed," but it wasn't just about the food. It was a superlative happiness, a boundless love, a dismissal of other relations that distracted from our great familial love. That first turkey eaten just by us, as a family, was, I know it was, the beginning of a new, reconfigured love, fuller, richer, freer, more complacent and gentler with itself. And so was born in our family a happiness that—well, who am I to say, others may have felt a happiness as great—but that I can't imagine any could be any greater.

Mom ate so much turkey that at one point I thought, she's going to feel sick. But then I thought, let her! Even if she keels over, at least once in her life she'll have truly eaten turkey!

These were the heights of selflessness to which I'd been elevated by our immense love . . . Afterward, there were some grapes and some cookies, the ones that back home they call "happy couples." But not even that dangerous association brought up the memory of my father, converted by the turkey into a dignified figure, a sublime object of contemplation.

We left the table. It was almost two in the morning, all of us happy, a little giddy after two bottles of beer. Everyone was off to bed, to sleep or to toss and turn, who cares. Even a sleepless night can be good, as long as it's a happy one. The trouble was Rose, who was Catholic before being Rose, and had promised to wait up for me with a bottle of champagne. To get out of the house, I lied, said I was going to a friend's party, kissed Mom with a wink, so's to let her know where I was really going and to give her a little something to worry about. The other two women I kissed, no winking. And now, Rose! . . .

LIMA BARRETO (1881–1922) was a satirical author and journalist from Rio de Janeiro. He is best known for his serialized 1911 novel *The Sad End of Policarpo Quaresma*, which criticized the First Brazilian Republic. In later years, Barreto suffered from depression and alcoholism and died of a heart attack at forty-one years old.

OLAVO BILAC (1865–1916) was a Brazilian poet of the Parnassian tradition. He was a founding member of the Brazilian Academy of Letters and is known as the "Prince of Brazilian Poets." In addition to poetry, Bilac also wrote textbooks, essays, and advertising copy, and translated from German.

RUBEM BRAGA (1913–1990) was a Brazilian writer of short prose sketches. After attending law school, Braga served as a war correspondent in Italy during World War II. During his long career, Braga contributed to newspapers in São Paulo and Rio de Janeiro. His best known collections include *The Count and the Bird*, *The Grumbling Man*, and *The Yellow Butterfly*, from which the story in this volume is taken.

PAULO COELHO (1947–) was born in Rio de Janeiro. A troubled and rebellious teenager, at seventeen Paulo Coelho was committed to an asylum where he underwent electroshock therapy. This difficult experience formed the foundation of his novel *Veronika Decides to Die*. After his release, Paulo Coelho traveled the world, then worked in music as a songwriter, producer, and record executive. He is the author of twenty-two international bestsellers and is best known for his novel *The Alchemist*.

CUTI (1951–) is the pseudonym of Luiz Silva. With a master's degree and a doctorate in Brazilian literature from the Instituto de Estudos da Linguagem at Unicamp, he is a founding member of the literary group Quilombhoje and of the journal *Cadernos Negros*, contributing to forty-four of its forty-five issues. He has published poetry collections, short story collections, as well as scholarly and theatrical works.

ST. JOSÉ DE ANCHIETA (1534–1597) was a Jesuit missionary to Brazil who was instrumental in founding the cities of São Paulo and Rio de Janeiro. Born in the Canary Islands and considered the father of Brazilian literature, he composed poems and plays and wrote the first grammar of the Tupí language. He was canonized by Pope Francis in 2014.

MÁRIO DE ANDRADE (1893–1945) was a Brazilian novelist, poet, and musicologist deeply involved in the avant-garde movement in São Paulo. He was instrumental in the 1922 São Paulo arts festival Modern Art Week. Andrade's 1928 novel *Macunaíma*, drawing on his research into indigenous Brazilian music, folklore, and culture, was one of the foundational texts of Brazilian Modernism.

JOAQUIM MARIA MACHADO DE ASSIS (1839–1908), born and raised in Rio de Janeiro, is regarded by many as the greatest Brazilian writer. He was a founding member and the first president of the Brazilian Academy of Letters in 1897. The author of numerous novels, plays, poems, short story collections, and several translations, he is best known for his masterful novels *Dom Casmurro*, *The Posthumous Memoirs of Bras Cubas*, and *Quincas Borba*, and the short story "Midnight Mass," in this volume.

ALPHONSUS DE GUIMARAENS (1870–1921), born in Ouro Preto, Minas Gerais, was the pseudonym of Afonso Henrique da Costa Guimarães. He was a writer of mystical, symbolist poetry. His first works *Septenary of the Sorrows of Our Lady and the Chamber of Repose* (excerpted in this volume) and *Mystic Lady* were published in 1899. In addition to his poetic work, de Guimaraens translated poetry by Stephen Mallarmé and worked as a journalist and judge.

RACHEL DE QUEIROZ (1910–2003), born and raised in Fortaleza, Ceará, was a writer of the Northeastern school of Brazilian novelists. Queiroz was briefly a member of the Brazilian Communist Party but left due to its interference in writing. In addition to novels, she also published plays and was well known for her essays. She won the Jabuti and Camões prizes and in 1977 she became the first female writer to be admitted to the Brazilian Academy of Letters.

GONÇALVES DIAS (1823–1864) was a prominent poet and playwright of the Brazilian Romantic movement who is often considered Brazil's national poet. Born in Maranhão, Dias studied French, Latin, and philosophy before traveling to Portugal to earn a law degree. It was there that he wrote his most famous work, the poem *Exile Song.* Dias's poetic work was informed by his mixed European, African, and indigenous background.

VICTOR HERINGER (1988–2018) was an author of German descent, born in Rio de Janeiro and raised in Nova Friburgo. His debut novel *Impossible City* was published in 2009 and his second novel *Gloria* was awarded Brazil's Jabuti Prize. His 2016 novel *The Love of Singular Men* was nominated for numerous awards and its English translation was a finalist for the National Book Critics Circle's John Leonard Prize. Heringer also wrote poetry and essay collections.

TERRI HINTE (1951–) is a native New Yorker who has been based in the San Francisco Bay Area for more than fifty years, pursuing a career as a music publicist as well as a writer and editor. She has represented hundreds of jazz and Brazilian artists. She lives in Richmond, California.

RONA JAFFE (1931–2005) was an American novelist born in Brooklyn and raised on Manhattan's Upper East Side. After graduating from Radcliffe College, Jaffe worked as an editor. Her first novel, *The Best of Everything*, was published in 1958 and made into a feature film. Jaffe contributed cultural articles to *Cosmopolitan* and published over ten more novels, as well as a collection of short stories.

CLARICE LISPECTOR (1920–1977) was a Ukrainian-born Brazilian novelist and short story writer. Lispector grew up in Recife and Rio de Janeiro and began publishing short stories and journalistic pieces while a law student. Her debut novel, *Near to the Wild Heart*, published in 1943, was a sensation and won the prestigious Graça Aranha Prize. Her works include nine novels and nine short story collections, as well as children's literature, journalism, and over thirty-five translations from English and French.

BRUNA DANTAS LOBATO (1991–), born in Natal, Brazil, is the author of *Blue Light Hours* and an assistant professor of English and creative writing at Grinnell College. Her translation of *The Words That Remain* by Stênio Gardel won the National Book Award for Translated Literature.

PATRÍCIA MELO (1962–) is a highly regarded novelist, playwright and scriptwriter. She has been awarded Brazil's 2001 Jabuti Prize and the 2013 German LiBeraturpreis. In 2023, her book *The Simple Art of Killing a Woman* was nominated for the Prix Fémina in the category Best Foreign Novel. The novel won the INDIES Book of the Year Awards 2023 in the United States and the Grand Prix Héroïne Madame Figaro 2024 in France.

COELHO NETO (1864–1934) was a writer, politician, and professor, who founded and occupied the second chair of the Brazilian Academy of Letters. Of mixed Portuguese and indigenous heritage, Coelho Neto studied medicine and law in São Paulo and Recife and was involved in abolitionist and republican causes. He wrote over fifty novels, short story collections, plays, as well as stories and theatrical works for children.

GRACILIANO RAMOS (1892–1953) was a Brazilian novelist whose works centered on the northeast area of Brazil where he spent most of his life. He is well known for his novels *São Bernardo*, *Anguish*, and *Barren Lives*. He also wrote short stories, children's books, and memoirs, including a posthumously published work detailing ten months he spent in prison during the dictatorship of Getúlio Vargas. He became a member of the Communist Party of Brazil in 1945.

LUIZ RUFFATO (1961–) was born in Cataguases, Minas Gerais, and is the author of several novels and many short stories. He has received Brazilian national prizes including the Machado de Assis Prize, the São Paulo Art Critic's Association Award, and the Jabuti Prize, as well as the Cuban Casa de las Américas Prize.

MOACYR SCLIAR (1937–2011), born in Porto Alegre, Rio Grande do Sul, was a prolific writer and physician. Much of his fiction is centered on Jewish life in Brazil and one of his novels was featured in the National Yiddish Book Center's list of the 100 Greatest Works of Modern Jewish Literature. His works include collections of short stories and essays, novels, autobiographical writings, and children's books.

LYGIA FAGUNDES TELLES (1918–2022) was a lawyer and a highly–regarded Brazilian novelist, journalist, and short story writer. She received the Coelho Neto Prize from the Brazilian Academy of Letters, multiple awards from the São Paulo Association of Art Critics, the Arthur Azevedo Prize, the Jabuti Prize, and many other awards. She was the third woman to be elected to the Brazilian Academy of Letters and in 2016, she became the first Brazilian woman to be nominated for the Nobel Prize in Literature.

VIRGÍLIO VÁRZEA (1863–1941) was the son of a sailor and, after attending the Naval Academy in Rio de Janeiro, he left to sail the world, visiting Uruguay, Argentina, Cabo Verde, and South Africa as well as parts of Europe and the Indian Ocean. Returning to Brazil, Várzea studied journalism and literature. He wrote a history of Ilha de Santa Catarina, where he lived for many years, as well as many stories and essays.

LUIS FERNANDO VERISSIMO (1936–) is best known as an essayist and author of humorist texts written for Brazilian newspapers and magazines. He is also a cartoonist, translator, and novelist.

"It's Christmas Night and I'm All Alone"
"The Christmas Turkey"
TRANSLATED BY JULIANA BARBASSA

"The Nativity of Jesus" (originally written in Latin)
TRANSLATED BY ODILE CISNEROS
FROM THE PORTUGUESE BY ARMANDO CARDOSO, S.J.

"José's Sandals"
TRANSLATED BY MARGARET JULL COSTA

"Midnight Mass"
"My Christmas"
TRANSLATED BY MARGARET JULL COSTA AND ROBIN PATTERSON

"Feast Day"
TRANSLATED BY RALPH EDWARD DIMMICK

"The Peal of Bells at Christmas"
TRANSLATED BY ELOAH F. GIACOMELLI

"A Christmas Miracle"
TRANSLATED BY FRANCIS K. JOHNSON

"Christmas on the Ferry"
"The Atheist"
"A Christmas Story"
"Christmas Chronicle"
TRANSLATED BY SOPHIE GRACE LELLMAN

"Christmas Sonnet"
TRANSLATED BY ANA LESSA-SCHMIDT

"Merry Christmas"
TRANSLATED BY SOPHIE LEWIS

"Christmas" by Ovalo Bilac
"Hymn of the Three Magi"
"Second Pang"
TRANSLATED BY MARK LOKENSGARD

"The Doll"
TRANSLATED BY ANDREW MCDOUGALL

"The Parish Priest"
"Christmas" by Virgílio Várzea
TRANSLATED BY KIM OLSON

"Pax Domestica"
TRANSLATED BY JAMES YOUNG

A VERY INDIAN CHRISTMAS

This anthology captures the distinctive magic of Christmas in India and in the Indian diaspora with a splendid collection of essays, stories, poems, and hymns—both in English and translated from India's other languages. It includes works by Nobel laureate Rabindranath Tagore, Booker Prize winners Salman Rushdie and Aravind Adiga, Pulitzer Prize winner Jhumpa Lahiri, Khushwant Singh, Jerry Pinto, Damodar Mauzo, Vivek Menezes, Hansda Sowvendra Shekhar, and others.

A VERY GERMAN CHRISTMAS

This collection brings together traditional and contemporary holiday stories from Austria, Switzerland and Germany. You'll find classic works by the Brothers Grimm, Johann Wolfgang von Goethe, Heinrich Heine, Thomas Mann, Rainer Maria Rilke, Hermann Hesse, Joseph Roth and Arthur Schnitzler, as well as more recent tales by writers like Heinrich Böll, Peter Stamm and Martin Suter.

A VERY MEXICAN CHRISTMAS

A Very Mexican Christmas is sure to delight, warm, and astonish by turns. You'll find spellbinding work by some of Mexico's most important writers, including Carlos Fuentes, bestselling Laura Esquivel, and other contemporary favorites like Amparo Dávila, Sandra Cisneros, Fabio Morábito, and Carmen Boullosa, as well as fresh translations of classics by Sor Juana Inés de la Cruz, Amado Nervo, and Ignacio Manuel Altamirano.

A VERY SCANDINAVIAN CHRISTMAS

The best Scandinavian holiday stories including classics by Hans Christian Andersen, Nobel Prize winner Selma Lagerlöf, August Strindberg as well as popular Norwegian author Karl Ove Knausgaard. These Nordic tales—coming from the very region where much traditional Christmas imagery originates—convey a festive spirit laden with lingonberries, elks, gnomes and aquavit in abundance. A smorgasbord of unexpected literary gifts sure to provide plenty of pleasure and *hygge*, that specifically Scandinavian blend of coziness and contentment.

A VERY FRENCH CHRISTMAS

This brings together the best French Christmas stories of all time in an elegant and vibrant collection featuring classics by Guy de Maupassant and Alphonse Daudet, plus stories by the esteemed twentieth century author Irène Némirovsky and contemporary writers Dominique Fabre and Jean-Philippe Blondel. With a holiday spirit conveyed through sparkling Paris streets, opulent feasts, wandering orphans, flickering desire, and more than a little wine, this collection proves that the French have mastered Christmas.

A VERY ITALIAN CHRISTMAS

This volume brings together the best Italian Christmas stories of all time in a fascinating collection featuring classic tales and contemporary works. With writing that dates from the Renaissance to the present day, from Boccaccio to Pirandello, as well as Anna Maria Ortese, Natalia Ginzburg and Nobel laureate Grazia Deledda, this choice selection delights and intrigues. Like everything the Italians do, this is Christmas with its very own verve and flair, the perfect literary complement to a *Buon Natale italiano*.

A VERY RUSSIAN CHRISTMAS

This is Russian Christmas celebrated in supreme pleasure and pain by the greatest of writers, from Dostoevsky and Tolstoy to Chekhov and Teffi. The dozen stories in this collection will satisfy every reader, and with their wit, humor, and tenderness, packed full of sentimental songs, footmen, whirling winds, solitary nights, snow drifts, and hopeful children, the collection proves that Nobody Does Christmas Like the Russians.

A VERY IRISH CHRISTMAS

This collection transports readers to the Emerald Isle with stories and poems sure to bring holiday cheer. The anthology is packed with beloved classics, forgotten treasures, and modern masterpieces. You'll find wondrous works by James Joyce, Elizabeth Bowen, W. B. Yeats, Anne Enright, William Trevor, Colm Tóibín, Bernard MacLaverty and many more.

ONE FOR EACH NIGHT

This rich medley of stories, poems, and essays features evocations of Chanukah by classic and contemporary authors including Sholom Aleichem, Nobel laureates S. Y. Agnon and Elie Wiesel, I. L. Peretz, Emma Lazarus, Theodor Herzl, Chaim Potok, Mark Strand, A. B. Yehoshua, Emma Green, Joanna Rakoff, and Rebecca Newberger Goldstein.

THE 6:41 TO PARIS *by Jean-Philippe Blondel*
Cécile, a stylish 47-year-old, has spent the weekend visiting her parents outside Paris. By Monday morning, she's exhausted. These trips back home are stressful and she settles into a train compartment with an empty seat beside her. But it's soon occupied by a man she recognizes as Philippe Leduc, with whom she had a passionate affair that ended in her brutal humiliation 30 years ago. In the fraught hour and a half that ensues, Cécile and Philippe hurtle towards the French capital in a psychological thriller about the pain and promise of past romance.

THE BISHOP'S BEDROOM *by Piero Chiara*
World War Two has just come to an end and there's a yearning for renewal. A man in his thirties is sailing on Lake Maggiore in northern Italy, hoping to put off the inevitable return to work. Dropping anchor in a small, fashionable port, he meets the enigmatic owner of a nearby villa. The two form an uneasy bond, recognizing in each other a shared taste for idling and erotic adventure. A sultry, stylish psychological thriller executed with supreme literary finesse.

THE ANIMAL GAZER *by Edgardo Franzosini*
A hypnotic novel inspired by the strange and fascinating life of sculptor Rembrandt Bugatti, brother of the fabled automaker. Bugatti obsessively observes and sculpts the baboons, giraffes, and panthers in European zoos, finding empathy with their plight and identifying with their life in captivity. Rembrandt Bugatti's work, now being rediscovered, is displayed in major art museums around the world and routinely fetches large sums at auction. Edgardo Franzosini recreates the young artist's life with intense lyricism, passion, and sensitivity.

To purchase these titles and for more information please visit newvesselpress.com.